The Brick House Burglars

Also by Peni R. Griffin

The
Brick House
Burglars

Peni R. Griffin

Margaret K. McElderry Books
New York
Maxwell Macmillan Canada
Toronto
Maxwell Macmillan International
New York • Oxford • Singapore • Sydney

For Dad, who won't really approve

Margaret K. McElderry Books   Maxwell Macmillan Canada, Inc.
Macmillan Publishing Company   1200 Eglinton Avenue East
866 Third Avenue   Suite 200
New York, NY 10022   Don Mills, Ontario M3C 3N1

Macmillan Publishing Company is part of the Maxwell Communication
Group of Companies.
First edition
Printed in the United States of America
10 9 8 7 6 5 4 3 2 1
The text of this book is set in 11-point Bookman Light.
Library of Congress Cataloging-in-Publication Data
Griffin, Peni R.
The Brick House Burglars / Peni R. Griffin. — 1st ed.
p.   cm.
Summary: A group of kids from a run-down neighborhood start
using an old mansion for a club house and soon discover some
mysterious goings-on involving a plot to destroy the mansion for the
insurance money.
ISBN 0-689-50579-5
[1. Mystery and detective stories.   2. Clubs—Fiction.   3. City and
town life—Fiction.]   I. Title.
PZ7.G88136Br   1994

Contents

Chapter One / Breaking In   1
Chapter Two / The Brick House   9
Chapter Three / Fights   19
Chapter Four / Becoming Burglars 28
Chapter Five / Meetings   38
Chapter Six / Matches   46
Chapter Seven / Detectives   51
Chapter Eight / Jobs   61
Chapter Nine / Suspicions   71
Chapter Ten / Things Look Bad   80
Chapter Eleven / Donnavita Detects 89
Chapter Twelve / The Second Fire 98
Chapter Thirteen / Rainbow Detects 106
Chapter Fourteen / Stakeout   113
Chapter Fifteen / Accusations   121
Chapter Sixteen / End Pending   130

CHAPTER ONE
Breaking In

THE FIRST THING I WANT TO SAY IS, I DON'T THINK I should be the one writing this. I'm only one of us that did all this. Mr. Sanchez says the important thing is to get someone who can put the right words in the right order, though, and that's me. Plus, Heather and Donnavita and Rainbow all say no way are they going to write on something this long. So . . .

The Brick House is on the corner where we get off the city bus from school. It's two story, pinkish brick, with a pillared front porch, a screened back porch, two bay windows stacked on top of each other, and a dormer. A bay window is the kind where a three-sided piece of wall pokes out with the sides angled and a window in each side, and a dormer sticks out from the roof. All the first-floor windows are boarded up and burglar barred, the paint's coming off the pillars, the yard's all weeds, and the whole thing's surrounded by a chain-link fence. On the side facing the bus stop, the chain link is on top of a brick wall. This day I'm talking about, when we got off the bus, we saw that somebody had spray painted "Los Red Dukes" along this wall and dirty words across the sign that told people interested in buying the house to call Weller & Weller Co.

"That stupid Jimmy Losoya," said Heather, looking at the dirty words. "You'd think he'd have something better to do."

The right word for Heather is cool. She had mono so bad when she was six that she couldn't go to school, so she's a year older than us even though she's in the same grade, but she doesn't act like she's ever been held back. She stands straight and talks straight, and even when I know for a fact that her clothes came out of the Goodwill, they look brand new.

"We don't know for a fact it was Jimmy," said Rainbow, who lives next door to him, "but it probably was."

The right word for Rainbow is little. She's two months older and six inches shorter than me. Her clothes look like they come from the Goodwill, even when they're brand new. (Mom says that's mean, but Rainbow says it's true and leave it in.)

Donnavita went around to the front of the house, which faces the side street. She leaned on the pad-locked gate, next to the No Trespassing sign, and gazed up at the second floor. The word for Donnavita is exotic. Her dad's mostly Italian and her mom is part Mexican and part Chinese. She's got the most gorgeous eyes, and hair down to her knees almost. Someday she'll be the richest model in the world. "Those bay windows have window seats," she said, "and you can lift the seats like lids and it's hollow inside, like a chest."

"We can keep your model portfolios in it, when you get some," I said. I forgot to tell you, my name is Mary Jane. The right word for me is ordinary. I wish it wasn't, but it is.

"And the cushions can have roses embroidered all over them," said Rainbow.

"You always want to put roses on everything," said Donnavita. "Let's have morning glories."

"Bluebonnets," I said.

"Butterflies," said Heather, firmly, settling it, "and curtains to match. It's a shame there aren't more bay windows. Then we could each have a window seat for our stuff."

"Two of us can have the one upstairs, and the other two the one downstairs," suggested Rainbow.

"The downstairs one doesn't have a window seat," I said. I've lived in our apartment buildings two years longer than anybody else, because my mom is the manager, and I've had lots more time to play this game than they have. "The one downstairs is where the table goes. Like a breakfast nook."

"Dining rooms don't go in the fronts of houses," said Heather. "That's the living room."

"No, you go straight into the living room from the front door, and it runs all the way to the back of the house," I said.

"Bull," said Heather. "The living room runs across the front of the house and the kitchen and dining room are side by side in the back."

"Look, there's Isis," said Rainbow.

We stopped arguing and started trying to attract the cat's attention. "Hi, Isis. Pretty Isis." That kind of thing. She came out from under the front porch and looked at us, just the tip of her tail moving. She's black except for a white spot on her chest, and when she moved into the Brick House before school started she was fat and nervous. Now she was skinny and nervous. Rainbow's the one who named her Isis, which is from "Star Trek." Rainbow's mom is real big on the old "Star Trek" show and can talk out whole episodes, even though they don't have a TV.

Rainbow's also the one who carries food. She opened her purse and took out a baggie with a leftover drumstick in it. (Rainbow's mom fries a whole chicken every Sunday and they eat on the leftovers all the rest of the week. Rainbow says, once she grows up, she'll never eat chicken again.) She knelt on the sidewalk and held the drumstick up to the chain links. "Come on, Isis," she crooned. "Look what I've got for you."

"You shouldn't give cats chicken bones," I said.

"It's all I've got," said Rainbow.

Isis's nose twitched, but she didn't come any closer, just swung her tail harder. "Poke it through the

4

fence," said Heather. "You know she won't come up to us."

"She might someday," said Rainbow, poking the drumstick through. Isis came two steps closer. We all backed off, pretending not to watch. Isis slunk closer, as if she expected the old dry weeds to hide her, picked up the drumstick, and walked around the corner of the house.

"What's she doing?" asked Donnavita. "Why not eat it here?"

We followed her. That side of the house has a row of live oaks between the fence and the driveway that leads into the apartments' parking lot. We walked the fence line, and the cat walked the house line. "She's taking it to her kittens," I said.

"Under the screen porch," said Donnavita, smugly. We'd had bets on where the kittens were. "I told you."

You can tell that the screen porch on the back of the house comes off the kitchen because of the utility meters next to it. It's set sideways to the rest of the house and sticks out on the side nearest to the apartments, so it's really about a yard wider than the house. It's mostly windows with no glass, just screens. The screens are held tight by built-on frames with narrow sills. Sorry to go on and on about it, but it's kind of important.

With the drumstick dangling from the side of her mouth, Isis climbed up the gas meter, to the sill of one of the screens, up the screen, to the porch roof, to the broken window in the second story, and inside. We all

5

looked at one another and laughed. "She fooled us, all right," said Rainbow.

Heather leaned on the fence, looking over the route Isis had taken as if she were measuring it. "You know," she said, "I bet we could get in the same way."

"We can't go in there," I said.

"Not can't," said Donnavita. "Aren't supposed to."

My stomach started to hurt. "Somebody'd see us."

"No, they wouldn't," said Heather, turning around to check out the area. "The part of the porch that sticks out would hide us from the parking lot. These trees hide us from the driveway and your apartment. The house hides us from the main street and nobody uses this side street this time of day. The only time anybody might see us is while we're getting in the window."

Donnavita put her toes through a chain link. "And this fence is mega-easy to climb."

I looked at Rainbow. Her eyes were all wide and shiny, and she was already putting her books on the ground. "I'm smallest," she said. "I get to go first."

"Right," I said, "and if you fall through the porch roof and break your neck, the rest of us'll know not to follow you."

"Oh, come on," said Donnavita, also putting her books down.

"Rats," I said. "Mice. Cockroaches."

"Heck, we've got cockroaches in the apartments," said Rainbow. "And Isis has had lots of time to take care of rats and mice. You want to see the kittens, don't you?"

"And the rooms?" Donnavita was already starting to climb.

"Hold on," said Heather, and for a minute I had hope; but what she said was: "We've got to do this right. If we leave our books and purses here, they might get ripped off. Let's put them away and change out of our school clothes and meet back here in"—she looked at her watch—"fifteen minutes. And bring your jump ropes. If anybody's around we can jump till they go away."

This is supposed to be the truth, the whole truth, and nothing but the truth. So. We all knew better than to do this. We'd all, except maybe Rainbow, been told not to go into the Brick House. Even Rainbow could see the No Trespassing sign on the gate. To stop this, all I had to do was let on to my mom, who as apartment manager is always somewhere around; but I didn't. And we were all back at the live oaks in fifteen minutes, with our jeans on and our jump ropes in our hands.

I was still pretending to myself that I wasn't going in, though. I stood watch while the others climbed the fence. Then I climbed the fence, while Rainbow climbed onto the meter. I could see the parking lot better from on top of the fence, you see. The windowsill, even though it was real narrow, was sturdy, and with a boost from Heather, Rainbow was able to get to the roof. She waited on the edge till I gave her the all-clear sign, then she crawled lickety-split across the shingles and in at the window. Heather went next; then Donnavita; then I was alone on the fence.

I figured I could stay there and attract attention, or I could go home and watch TV, or I could go see the kittens and the inside of the Brick House.

So I went in.

CHAPTER TWO
The Brick House

THE CLIMB WAS EASIER THAN IT SOUNDS. I WAS
sure Mom would look out, or somebody'd come into
the parking lot, during the two seconds it took to get
from the corner of the roof to the window, but nothing
happened. The only glass left in the window was a big
curved piece in the top, and I ducked under that with
no problem, though I could imagine it dropping like
the guillotine in a movie I once saw about the French
Revolution.

"It's Swahili for *star*," Rainbow was saying when I
came in.

"Since when do you speak Swahili?" Donnavita
asked.

"It's in one of Domie's books." (Domie is short for

Freedom, Rainbow's mom's name.) "It's Uhura's first name."

Heather groaned. "One cat named after 'Star Trek' is enough."

The room was as big as Rainbow's apartment, about twice as high, and had four windows. There was a mattress with the stuffing coming out in the middle of the floor, built-in shelves, and green wallpaper with yellow roses. We squatted in a line by the window, watching Isis and the kittens. Isis watched us back. The kittens fought over the drumstick. One was like Isis, black with a white star, two were calico, and one was yellow tabby. They were unsteady on their feet, but they could sure eat chicken.

"Don't you think Nyota's a pretty name?" Rainbow asked me.

"Don't you think Rainbow's had her turn naming cats?" asked Donnavita.

"I don't see what difference it makes," I said. "There are four kittens, and four of us."

"That's true," said Heather, "but what if we both want to name the same kitten? I say we draw straws for first pick."

"We don't have any straws," said Rainbow.

"So we do it later." Heather made a motion with one hand, like she was tossing the subject over her shoulder. "Hey, look at that one with the white feet! He's swallowing whole."

We could tell Isis wouldn't let us get any closer to her babies than we already were, but that was still closer

10

than we'd ever been to kittens before. They were neat, but I kept looking at the house, too. I'd been making up how this house looked inside for so long, I couldn't believe I was really in it.

This room had two doors, a closed one in the wall opposite the broken window, and one standing open into the hall. The floor was made of wood the color of the honey Domie buys at the health food store—gold clover honey with streaks of brown buckwheat honey. Through the hall door I could see a railing, and the top of the stairs. What was it like at the bottom? I wondered. What was it like down the hall, in the room with the top bay window?

The kittens wouldn't come near us, and after a while they had polished off the chicken and started playing with the bone. "You'd better take it away from them, Rainbow," I said. "They could break it open and choke to death on the splinters." My mom had a dog when she was little that died from eating chicken bones.

So Rainbow crawled forward, talking in a quiet, soothing voice. Isis growled, and all the kittens ran to the mattress and clawed their way into the hole; but they kept their heads out to watch. Isis got between them and Rainbow while she picked up the bone and promised to bring more.

Meanwhile Heather walked around the room. She ran her hand along the built-in shelves, and opened the closed door. "Just a closet," she said.

I went to the open door. The stairs came up in the middle of the hall, with a railing to keep people from falling through. On the left was an open door showing a bathroom; down the hall to my right and at the end of the hall were two closed doors. The stairs went down into shadow. "You know, y'all, as long as we're trespassing anyway, it won't hurt to look around," I said.

"Of course it won't," said Heather, coming up behind me. She led the way down the hall.

The second bedroom wasn't as nice as Isis's, because it only had two windows, but it also had built-in shelves, and its wallpaper was green, with horses. We argued about whether it had belonged to a boy or to a horse-crazy girl, but couldn't decide. We agreed that Isis's room had belonged to a teenage girl, the kind who has dates and a vanity table.

The front room went all across the front of the house, the wallpaper was faded silver with a lattice pattern, the bay window had a window seat just like Donnavita's made-up one, and there was a fireplace in the corner! We'd figured on a fireplace downstairs, because we could see the chimney, but a fireplace in the bedroom was better than we'd ever dreamed!

The only trouble with this room was the windows all around three walls. If we'd belonged here they would have been cool, but we didn't want anybody to see us from the street, so we had to crawl along the floor to get to the window seat. Donnavita got to look inside first, because it'd been her idea. I would've been afraid to, anyway. What if it had rats inside? But it let a cool, fresh smell into our faces.

"It's lined with cedar," said Donnavita, rubbing the smooth, red wood. "My mom has cedar blocks she puts in our drawers to keep the moths out. Maybe they kept quilts in here."

"The old lady who lived here did have quilts," I said. "When she died her kids had a sale, and there was a whole stack."

Heather was eye-measuring the window seat. "You know," she said, "there'd be room in here for each of us to keep stuff."

"We've got places to keep stuff at home," I said.

"Not private places. Let's look downstairs."

Downstairs was spooky and dark, because of the windows being boarded up so only a little light came in through the tops. Heather turned out to be right about the layout; the front door opened into the hall, which led straight back to the dining room, and the bay window and fireplace were in the living room. Instead of doorways, this room and the dining room had archways. The ceilings were not only high down here, they had fancy molded designs in the corners and around the light fixtures; but we couldn't tell what the designs were in the dim light.

The kitchen was sad and messy, with gas and water pipes sticking out of the floors where the stove and sink had been. The linoleum was all torn up, and holes in the floor and walls looked like good places for rats. Rainbow opened two doors under the stairs, finding a closet and a powder room with the fixtures ripped out. Someone had left a roll of carpet in the closet.

I was beginning to feel queasy. "It's too spooky down here," I said. "Let's go look at the kittens some more."

"Yeah, we need a flashlight," said Heather.

"Don't you wish we could live like this?" said Donnavita, trailing upstairs in this dreamy model way she does sometimes.

"Not enough rooms to go around," said Rainbow.

"I don't mean all of us together, dummy. I mean each of us have a house like this. In my family I'd probably get stuck with the middle bedroom, but even that's better than what I've got now." Donnavita shares a room with her big sister.

"Just one of these floors would be better than what I've got now," said Rainbow. She sleeps in the living room with her mom.

"I bet Marshall wouldn't mind if I had the back bedroom," said Heather. Marshall is her big brother.

"No way would Sloop get first pick," I said. "That back bedroom is mine!" Sloop is my little brother.

The kittens were out playing again, and when we came into the room they ran for the mattress; but in a little while the yellow one came back out and pounced on Isis's tail while she was twitching it at us. She bopped him over on his back and started washing him. The calico with the white feet snuck up on her then, and pretty soon they were playing just like we weren't around. We watched them and talked about their names some more.

After a while we decided we'd better get out before

14

people started coming home from work. Heather went first, then Rainbow, then Donnavita, then me.

When we were safe on the driveway, Heather said slowly, "You know, I don't see where it would hurt anything if we kept a few private things in that window seat."

"I didn't see any rats," said Donnavita, "or broken boards, or anything like that."

"And somebody ought to feed those kittens," said Rainbow.

I felt sick, and tingly—the tingly you feel on Christmas Eve. "Get real," I said. "Sooner or later somebody'd see us."

"I don't see why, if we're careful," said Heather. "Practically the only place you can see that window from is the parking lot. As long as we time it so we're not inside when people start coming home from work, we should be just fine."

"We'd be burglars," I said.

"No, trespassers," said Donnavita. "We wouldn't steal anything. Just borrow the house for a while."

"That's just as bad!"

"No, it's not," said Rainbow. "We're not hurting anything."

Heather started jumping her rope. "If the owners cared anything about the Brick House, they'd be using it," she said.

"The owners are my mom's bosses," I said.

"Then they owe us," said Heather. "If they'd made a playground, we wouldn't need the Brick House."

"It's dangerous," I said, desperately.

"Not as dangerous as playing in the parking lot," said Heather, skipping away. "Look, you don't have to come with us if you don't want. You can't help it if you're chicken."

I have sat here and looked at this page for five minutes trying to think of the right words to say how bad I felt then, while Donnavita and Rainbow started skipping their ropes and Heather started chanting a new rhyme she'd learned. I feel bad again when I think about it, but it's too complicated to describe. I started jumping rope, too.

> *Had a little candy store,*
> *Couldn't make it pay.*
> *Asked my boyfriend what to do.*
> *He told me right away.*

"Look out!" said Rainbow. "Car coming!"

We skipped out of the way. We're good at that. It was Mr. Sanchez's car, a beat-up gold Chevy.

> *Take a can of gasoline,*
> *Spill it on the floor,*
> *Take a match, give a scratch,*
> *No more candy store.*

"Hey!" Donnavita missed a step. "Roxanne's with him!"

The right word for Mr. Sanchez is hunk. None of us is boy crazy, but you don't have to be to think that about Mr. Sanchez. He came to our school once for a fire-safety demo, because he's a firefighter, and all the girls were jealous of us for living so near him. Donnavita's big sister, Roxanne, thinks he hung the moon in the sky; but even though she was sitting in the front seat with him, she didn't look happy. She was hunched down and looking out the window, till she saw us, when she looked in her lap. Mr. Sanchez waved at us, but his smile wasn't as gleaming bright as usual. He parked in his space, walked around the car, and opened the door for Roxanne. Then he walked her to her door.

"I'd better go see what's happening," said Donnavita.

She ran across the parking lot and went in. We all stopped jumping and trailed after her, but we felt too shy to go up to the door. "Roxanne should've gotten home while we were in the Brick House," said Heather. "You think she's in trouble?"

"It must be pretty big trouble, for her to look so bummed sitting next to Mr. Sanchez," said Rainbow.

While we stood around talking, Jimmy Losoya came out. The right word for Jimmy is ba-a-ad. He's the leader of Los Red Dukes. When he fights with his mom you can hear it clear over at our apartment. People say he never takes off his leather jacket even when it's a hundred degrees out because he's covering the needle tracks on his arms from doing drugs. Anyway, he jumped on his motorcycle and revved the engine too loud a couple of dozen times, then roared away.

Heather slung her jump rope over her shoulder. "Y'all think about what you want to keep in the Brick House, and what you want to name the kittens. We'll draw straws tomorrow."

"I'll name the kittens with you," I said, "but I can't keep breaking into the Brick House."

Heather shrugged. "I expect we'll survive without you."

So I went inside, where Mom was cooking hamburgers I had no appetite for.

CHAPTER THREE
Fights

MOM SAYS NOT TO BITE THE HAND THAT FEEDS me, so I won't say what I think about our apartments. There's stuff I have to describe, though, to make clear what's going on.

First, these aren't apartments like you think of, blocks of tall buildings with tennis courts, a swimming pool, and like that. There are several buildings, but they're all one story. The only places to play are the parking lot and the sand heap out back, where somebody was going to build something and didn't.

The apartments come in three sizes. Rainbow and her mom and grandmom have the one-bedroom size. Donnavita, Roxanne, and their mom and dad have the two-bedroom size. Heather and I have the three-bedroom size. Except for the number of bedrooms they're all alike, with windowless kitchenettes, plywood paneling, and free cable hookup. Because Mom's the manager, we've got the nicest apartment, number 1A, the only apartment in A block. The rest of the building is party room and laundry room.

I came in feeling sick and mixed-up. If Mom had asked me what was wrong then, I'd've told her; but she was in the kitchenette and didn't see me well enough to notice. "Hi, honey," she said. "It's time to set the table. And Sloop's been real quiet the last little while; could you check on him?"

That didn't take long. I went into my room to put my jump rope away and there was Sloop. He'd pulled out all the drawers in my desk, and he was scribbling, in my notebooks, with my seven-color pen!

The right word for Sloop is pest.

I slapped him. He howled. "Shut up!" I shouted. He howled louder. Torn pages of notebook were all over the floor, and he had given a lavender face to the best princess I had ever drawn—Princess Annabelle-Ambergris-Alison Smythe. "Look what you did!" I shook him.

Mom came in. "What's all the noise about?"

"She hit me!" howled Sloop.

"I slapped him once," I said, "and he deserved it! Look at this!" I held up pages of notebook. He'd scribbled all over them, sometimes so hard that he tore the paper.

"I wanted to write a story like Mary Jane does!" I don't know how Sloop can talk and howl at the same time. Practice, I guess.

"You can't even write yet," I said.

"I can too." Sloop pointed to some red scribbles. "See? That says, 'Once upon a time there was a boy named Snoopy and he lived in a ice-cream factory.' "

Mom laughed and covered it up, but not fast enough. This always happens. She said, way too nicely, "But you shouldn't use other people's things without permission."

"I didn't think she'd mind," said Sloop. He gave me his big-eyed-orphan look. "I'm sorry, Mary Jane."

"Sorry isn't good enough," I said. With this on top of how bad I'd been feeling when I came in, I was about ready to cry.

"Sorry's all he can say," said Mom. "Come on, except for that one picture he seems to have only used blank pages. You can forgive him."

"No, I can't," I said. "Doesn't he even get a paddling?"

Right then something boiled over in the kitchenette, with a big hissing, and Mom had to run get it. Sloop just sat there, looking at me. "Get out of my room, John Burkholder Wilson," I said. (John Burkholder is Sloop's real name. Sloop is what you call an in-joke, because of this song about the sloop *John B.* on one of Dad's old records.) "And don't you ever come in here again!" I practically shoved him out, and slammed the door.

It was true, most of the pages he'd spoiled were blank, but I hate having pages torn out of spiral notebooks. Plus, he'd colored that princess's face, half torn out the last page of my story about the witch-cat, and broken the pen so that the green ink wouldn't write anymore. I had been going to make a whole book full of stories and pictures and poetry, and when the notebook was full I would get it published. I had been working on it all summer, and had even picked out a pen name—Mirabelle Winchester. Now it was all spoiled.

Dinner was awful. Dad worked late at the warehouse and came home griping about his boss and his sore feet. Mostly my dad is better than other people's dads, but when his boss and his feet are bugging him, he doesn't want to hear about anybody else's troubles. I didn't have any appetite, and Mom got on me for sulking and not making up with Sloop, who was being as angelic as he could to make me look bad. Then when I was putting my dishes in the dishwasher I dropped my favorite glass, the one with the old-fashioned Coke girl on it, and it broke all over the floor and I had to sweep it up.

Then the phone rang.

Mom answered it, and when she hung up she said to me, "Donnavita's coming over to do homework with you."

Usually this would've been okay, but tonight I was teed off already. "Since when?" I asked. "What if I don't want to do homework? What if I don't have any homework?"

"You stop that right now," said Mom. "Something's

going on over at the Barracottas tonight, and everybody's all upset."

"It's about that airhead Roxanne," I said.

"Oh? And what do you think you know about it?"

I told her about seeing Roxanne in Mr. Sanchez's car. Mom looked interested, but Dad said, "Whatever it is, it's not our business."

When Donnavita arrived she looked about how I'd felt earlier, all sick and excited. Mom and Dad didn't ask her anything, but she didn't waste any time once we got into my room. "Roxy's in such mega-trouble I practically feel sorry for her," she said, dumping her books on my bed.

"What happened?" I asked, getting on the bed with her and putting my head up close.

She put her forehead on mine and whispered loudly, "She set a rest room on fire at the high school!"

I goggled. (That means my eyes got wide and my mouth fell open and I looked really stupid, I was so surprised.) "What'd she do that for?"

"It was an accident," said Donnavita. "She didn't tell the school that, though. She said she did it to get out of a chemistry test."

"Why'd she say that if it was an accident?"

"Because she'd be in even worse trouble if she told the truth." Donnavita was feeling better, I could tell. "You got to promise not to tell this part."

I crossed my heart, hoped to die, stick a needle in my eye.

"She was smoking dope!" hissed Donnavita. "Or anyway, she was trying. A friend of hers scored a joint and—"

"Say what?"

"Scored a joint." Donnavita made an impatient motion, like I was supposed to know this already. "You know, that's what they call it when you buy one of those dope cigarettes. Anyway, her friend offered to share, and Roxanne was curious so she tried. But it didn't do either of them any good—all they did was choke and get a little dizzy. She says her eyes still itch. So she got disgusted and threw it away, only she threw it into the wastebasket instead of into the toilet. So that was all full of paper towels and stuff, and it started to smoke. So Roxanne ran out the door yelling 'Fire!' " Donnavita made a face. "And her friend disappeared. Roxanne won't tell on her, but she ought to. She doesn't owe anything to someone who ditched her."

"Why didn't she just say somebody else'd started the fire?"

"I think she must've had just enough dope to make her stupider than usual. She was mega-scared somebody'd go through the trash after the fire was out, and find the joint."

"So? It didn't have her name on it."

"I know, but . . ." Donnavita flapped her hands helplessly. "She said the first thing that came into her head, that she'd wanted to set the school on fire to get out of chemistry. She really hadn't studied for the test. But now all the teachers think she's a pyro."

"A what?"

"A pyro. Short for pyromaniac. That's what they call a crazy person who sets fires. So the teachers called the fire department, even though the fire was already out, and asked for somebody to talk to her."

"And that's how come she was riding with Mr. Sanchez?"

"Uh-huh. He volunteered when he heard who it was. Roxy started lying to him, too, but she'd totally lost it by that time, and was saying things that didn't make sense, so he knew something was wrong. And he started talking about how setting a fire is worse than taking a gun and shooting somebody, because the gun'll stop when you decide you're done, but a fire won't. If she'd set that school on fire, lots of people could've died, or been hurt, and the fire could've spread."

"So she told him about the dope so he wouldn't think she was worse than a murderer?"

Donnavita nodded. "I guess it's a little better for him to think she's stupid. Gramma says men like stupid women, anyway. You think that's true?"

"Maybe stupid men. Mr. Sanchez isn't stupid." Besides, Roxanne is way younger than him. She's only a sophomore (that's tenth grade). "So what happens to her now?"

"Well, he promised not to tell the school if she told

Mom and Dad. He sat and waited in the apartment till they got home to be sure she did it." Donnavita smiled. "Roxy kept wanting me to leave, but I wouldn't. We played crazy eights."

"I'm happy for you," I said. "What happens to her?"

"Practically nothing," said Donnavita. "Mom and Dad are still fighting with her, but I think the worst part was embarrassing herself in front of Mr. Sanchez, and that's all over. The school's making her take this fire-safety course, and she's grounded. And she's supposed to drop the friend that had the joint, but unless Roxanne tells on her we won't be able to tell if she does that or not."

After that we were able to do our homework. I helped her with history and she helped me with math. Donnavita works hard at math, because her mom says when she gets to be the richest model in the world, she'll need to be able to keep track of her own money so her managers won't rip her off. I showed her what Sloop had done to my pen and my notebook, too.

"When I grow up, I'm only going to have one kid," said Donnavita. "Brothers and sisters are too big a pain. Why don't you put your notebooks in the window seat? I'm going to keep my magazines and my model case there."

Donnavita scrounges magazines wherever she can, so she can copy the models' poses; and her model case is an old makeup kit of her mom's, where she's collected makeup and jewelry and stuff. "Won't Roxanne wonder where they've gone?" I asked.

"Naw. She's always dumping them on my bed and telling me to find someplace to put them that isn't in her way. If she doesn't see them, she won't think about them."

"I'd keep my story notebooks and my good pens and my diary there," I said, "if I were going to go with you."

"But why won't you?" asked Donnavita.

"You know we'd get skinned alive if we got caught."

"Why should we get caught? I don't think it's really dangerous a bit, and we're not hurting anything. You know your mom says it's a crime, that nice house sitting empty when folks could be using it."

"I know, but . . ." I wasn't sure how to finish the sentence.

"It's more your house than anybody's," Donnavita went on. "You're the one who started the game about how we'd fix it up if we could." She sprawled over the foot of the bed, checking my math answers. "Heather wants you to come, really."

I snorted. "She doesn't care."

"Yes, she does. It won't be as much fun without you, and she knows it."

I snorted again; but I felt good for the first time that evening.

CHAPTER FOUR

Becoming Burglars

JUST TO SHOW HOW EVERYTHING HAPPENS AT once, I heard fire trucks that night.

Actually, that isn't unusual. We aren't far from Mr. Sanchez's fire station. (Firefighters stay at the station day and night for a while, and then they're off duty for the same length of time. This is a major pain for their families, but Mr. Sanchez lives with Mr. Anstruther, who is an orderly at Santa Rosa Hospital and has hours that are just as big a pain, and they say it works out.) In the winter we might hear sirens two or three times a week, because people leave their space heaters on all night, and you shouldn't ever, ever do that. Also, homeless people break into the empty houses, to try and get warm, and they lose control of their campfires.

It was only October now, though, and we hadn't

heard the sirens for a long time. When I looked out my window the smoke was black, the sky was gray, and the glow was yellow-orange. I wondered what was burning.

We found out on the way to school. The bus passes an old adobe house, the kind people built when San Antonio was Spanish—maybe enough space for three rooms, a gallery along the front, and a tin roof. (Only I think when the Spanish built them they must've had tile roofs. I'm not sure.) It was closed off like the Brick House, with chain-link fence and No Trespassing and For Information Call Weller & Weller Co. signs, but it had been empty so long trees grew out the windows. The fence was so high even Jimmy Losoya hadn't been able to get in to spray paint the walls.

Not anymore. "Los Red Dukes" was sprayed in red on the walls. The roof was crumpled, the gallery poles had burned away, and the windows and door were empty holes surrounded by big, irregular black marks. "Wow," said Rainbow. "You wouldn't think adobe'd burn that much!"

"I guess there was a lot of wood inside," said Heather. "Paneling, and doors, and window frames."

"Gas lines," said Donnavita. "Electric wires."

"But how'd it get started?" I asked. "The gas and electricity'd be shut off."

Somebody'd been busy. "Los Red Dukes" had been scratched in the glass of the bus stop shelter where we got off and spray painted on the sidewalk and all over the walls of the buildings we passed. None of it'd been there yesterday. Rainbow looked at the graffiti and said, "You know, Jimmy didn't get home till after the fire. I heard his motorbike."

"People set fires on purpose, sometimes," I said.

"You think Los Red Dukes did it?" asked Donnavita.

"Why should they?" asked Rainbow.

"Who says they need a reason?" asked Heather.

Because the fire'd been so close to school, everybody talked about it. Somebody'd heard that the fire department said it was arson, which is what they call starting a fire on purpose. Everybody had a favorite suspect. There was a big fight during sixth-grade recess, because Kinny Jackson's big sister Dahomey had disappeared from high school yesterday, and somebody made a joke about her running away to be an arsonist. Late in the day somebody else said that Los Red Dukes had been arrested, but it wasn't true, because when we got home they were all in the parking lot, smoking and drinking plain-label beer. Rainbow had to walk past them to put her books away. She was scared to do it alone, so I went with her. They ignored us.

When we came out again Heather and Donnavita were already over by the Brick House with Heather's brother, Marshall. Marshall's older than Roxanne, but he's got problems. That's all Heather'll let you call it— not retarded or developmentally disabled. The right word for Marshall is determined. He goes to a special school where he's learning how to get a job.

"Did the fire scare y'all?" he asked when Rainbow and I came up. "It scared Heather."

"It did not!" Heather turned bright red.

"Then why didn't you want to go with me to see it?" he asked. "I went to see the fire. Heather couldn't stop me."

"Mom could've," said Heather. Her mom's a waitress at an all-night pancake house, and she'd been working the graveyard shift lately. That's what you call it when you start at midnight. So she hadn't been home. "If you go around telling people I was scared when I wasn't, I'll tell Mom you went out at night. You know we're not supposed to, and that's why I didn't go."

"You won't have to tell," said Donnavita. "It's not like Marshall could keep a secret. He'll tell on his ownself."

"I won't!" said Marshall. "I know lots of secrets!"

"Oh?" I said. "Like what?"

He laughed. "If I tell you, it won't be a secret." He wasn't always dumb.

Los Red Dukes were smoking and laughing. They made me nervous. I'd gotten my jump rope when I put my books away, so I started skipping. I must've had fires on the brain, because I started Heather's rhyme about the candy store. When I got to:

> Take a can of gasoline,
> Spill it on the floor,
> Take a match, give a scratch,
> No more candy store.

Jimmy stopped in the middle of a laugh and looked straight at me. Or seemed to. He was far enough away I couldn't see his face really. I kept on:

How much insurance did it pay?
One thousand, two thousand, three thousand—

Jimmy crushed his beer can and got up. All the Dukes had stopped laughing and were looking over toward us. I kept counting. Heather said, "What's the matter with them?"

"Maybe we should go in now," said Marshall.

"Six thousand, seven thousand, eight thousand," I counted.

The seven Dukes got on five motorbikes. You can't call them a cycle gang, because two of them don't have their own wheels and have to ride up behind. They didn't spend as much time revving as they usually do. Jimmy kick started his bike and came roaring straight at us by the time I got to "twenty thousand." I was off to the side, so I didn't move like the others did, but he swerved and I had to run on "twenty-one thousand."

We all screamed and scrambled for the live oaks. The other Dukes swerved at us, too, laughing meanly. All of us hid behind trees except for Marshall, who ran at them shouting, "Hey! You leave those kids alone! Hey!"

"It's okay, Marshall," said Heather as they roared down the street. "We're fine. They wouldn't really run over us."

Marshall shook his fist after them. "Stupid creeps! Picking on little girls! When that Jimmy comes back I'll—"

"You'll leave him alone," said Heather, laying down the law. "There are seven of them and only one of you. They could beat you up and then there wouldn't be anybody around to take care of me. You leave them alone till they really do something."

"Huh," said Marshall. "It won't be so easy to beat me up!"

"Isn't it almost time for that show you like?" asked Heather. "You'd better go inside before you miss it."

Marshall looked at his Kmart watch. "It's not even four yet. My cartoon's not on till four-thirty."

"Isn't there something on at four, though?" asked Donnavita.

He looked at her, frowning the way he does when he's thinking. "Y'all want to get rid of me," he said.

"Not get rid of exactly," said Heather. "There's girl stuff we want to do."

He thought some more and then smiled. "You got secrets."

"That's fair, isn't it?" Heather pointed out. "You've got secrets you wouldn't want us around for."

He nodded. "Yeah. That's fair. But you should say when you've got secrets. Not try to trick me. *That's* not fair."

"I'm sorry," said Heather. "Next time we'll say."

"Okay. I'll go inside now." He chuckled at us—that's

this low laugh he's got, that he usually does when he sees something funny but nobody else does—and loped off to the apartment. We watched to be sure he went in.

"All right," said Heather. "Y'all got your stuff for the window seat? And straws for naming the kittens?"

Donnavita held up her makeup kit and stack of magazines. "But how're we going to get them up there?" she asked. "We can't climb holding onto them."

Heather frowned and did her measuring bit. "What we need is something we can put it all in," she said. "You know, one of us kneel on the edge of the roof and one of us hand a bag up."

"Hang on," I said. "I'll see if I can borrow the backpack."

Mom was in the office, doing paperwork, with the doors open. Sloop and Cheryl, the little kid from 4B, played airplane in the party room. I told Mom we needed the backpack to play mountaineer with. A long time ago, somebody was going to build something behind our apartments, and they dumped a huge mound of that construction sand, which is so old now it has grass growing on it. We play there a lot in summer.

"That's fine," said Mom. "The pack's behind the vacuum in the hall closet."

"Me too! Me too!" shouted Sloop, grabbing on to my leg.

For a minute I was afraid Mom'd make me take him, but she said Sloop and Cheryl had to stay here so Cheryl's mom could find them, and I escaped before she could change her mind. I got the pack out of the closet, put my story notebook, my diary, and my seven-color pen in the bottom, and carried it out.

Nobody said anything about my things being in there but Heather smiled at me. Donnavita put her stuff in. Rainbow put in a diary that her mom'd been reading and putting helpful notes in, even though Rainbow kept telling her not to, and a Barbie doll some relative had given her. She was afraid Domie'd throw it out someday, because she kept complaining about how if you made a Barbie human-size the waist would be fifteen inches wide and the chest forty.

Heather had an album full of pictures made on the weekends she spends with her dad and a scrapbook of catalog pictures. We added some doll dishes and the food we'd scrounged for the kittens, and we were all set.

Rainbow went first and I was lookout again. Heather hoisted the pack up to Rainbow, who took it inside, and we climbed up one at a time after her without anyone seeing us. It wasn't as scary crawling under the broken glass this time.

Isis wasn't in the room, and the kittens scrambled for the mattress; but we set out the food in the doll dishes and sat down well away from them, and they soon got braver. Rainbow'd even saved her milk from lunch; they loved that. When Isis got there she was pretty ticked off, but it was too late by then. The kittens were never afraid of us again.

We drew straws to decide who got to pick the first name. The kittens wound up: Nyota (black), Sunshine (yellow), Boots (calico with white feet), and Bib (calico with white chest). After we settled that, Heather crossed her legs and banged her knee with her fist. "Hear ye, hear ye! This meeting is now in session!"

"What meeting?" I asked, at the same time that Rainbow said, "That's not what you say in meetings, silly; that's for courtrooms."

"It's meetings too," said Heather. "Don't you think we should have a club?"

"We've had so many clubs," Donnavita pointed out. "They never last more'n a week."

"That's because we never had a good place to hold meetings," said Heather. "We do now. You want to vote on officers?"

"What for?" I asked. "It always works out the same. You're president, Rainbow's vice president, Donnavita's treasurer, and I'm secretary. If I'd known this was going to be a meeting, I'd've brought a minutes book." Minutes are the notes about what went on in a meeting, and are the secretary's main job.

"What about that notebook in the pack?" asked Rainbow.

"That's for stories, but it'll do to start." Everybody waited while I dug it out. I turned it upside down and started at the back, so I'd have enough blank pages. "Old business," I said, "we named the kittens."

"We hadn't started the meeting yet," objected Rainbow.

"I think the meeting started when we got here," said

Heather. "Now the new business. We should have a name."

"The Secret Sharers," said Donnavita. (I found out later this is the title of a story in Roxanne's literature book.) "Or it could be Los Secret Sharers, if you wanted."

"Using *los* sounds too much like a gang," said Heather.

"The Secret Order of Isis," said Rainbow.

I scribbled fast to keep up, not really thinking, and the name popped into my head. "The Brick House Burglars," I said.

"We're not burglars," said Donnavita. "We're trespassers."

"Burglars sounds better," I said. "The *b*'s match."

That was all the names we came up with, so we voted. Heather's was the only vote that counted, because she was the only one who didn't have an idea of her own to vote for. She looked at all of us, and then said, "Brick House Burglars. We need to remember we could get into big trouble if we're caught. Being burglars will remind us to be careful."

I went to the top of the page (which since I'd turned the book upside down to start at the back was really the bottom) and squeezed in the title: Minutes of the Meetings of the Brick House Burglars.

"What about dues?" asked Donnavita.

37

CHAPTER FIVE
Meetings

WE SPENT A LOT OF THE REST OF THE MEETING arguing about dues. It's always a problem, because Rainbow doesn't get an allowance, and the rest of us get different amounts. I get a dollar a week; Heather gets twenty-five dollars a month from her dad; Donna-vita gets lunch money that she can save if she brings a sack lunch every day. Also, we each wanted to do different things with the money: buy cat food and milk, decorate Isis's room, buy a real notebook for the minutes, and like that.

We didn't really decide anything that day, but we stored our things in four stacks in the window seat and gave the three upstairs rooms official names—the Treasure Room, the Horse Room, and Isis's Room. Heather decided we ought to bring a flashlight and explore more downstairs; but it was getting on for suppertime, and we closed the meeting without arranging when to do that or whose flashlight to use.

That was Thursday. Friday we had another meeting, and decided to have "graduated dues." That was Donnavita's idea. She said she'd work out a scale based on how much we got, like income tax only simpler, and we'd each pay what we could afford. We also voted to buy the cat food first, because it's such a pain scrounging leftovers for the kittens. Then we played with the kittens and tried to get Isis to be friendly, but she wouldn't.

Saturday and Sunday are completely different from weekdays around our apartments. People are in and out all day, on their way shopping or to church or whatever. It was too dangerous to have a weekend meeting. Besides, Sunday I was rushing around. We had to get all of our errands out of the way, have supper early, and set up rows of folding chairs, and Mom made a big urn of coffee. Dad brought home three dozen doughnuts from the bakery thrift store, which got Sloop all excited; we had to tell him he could have one after his bath.

The word for the party room is drab. Except for a space at one end like a kitchenette, it's just a big square room with little windows and the same carpet and paneling as the apartments. It's a good place for tenants' meetings, because it's easy to remember what you don't like when you're in it.

This was going to be a big meeting. It was supposed

to start at seven o'clock, and at five minutes till we already had Mr. and Mrs. Barracotta (Donnavita's folks), and Mr. Sanchez and his roommate, Mr. Anstruther. Marshall came with his and Heather's mom, but Heather didn't. Mr. T. J. Weller, who owns the apartments along with his dad and who'd agreed to come, didn't show up till ten after.

It was still a little light out, and I was watching Sloop ride his trike. Mr. T. J. Weller pulled up in one of those expensive cars—a BMW. The right word for Mr. TJ is smooth—smooth blue suit, smooth tie, smooth hair, smooth voice; except today he had a little cold. He smiled. "Hi, Mary Jane," he said. He doesn't see me to talk to but once or twice a year, but he always remembers my name.

"Hi, Mr. Weller," I said.

"Now, Mr. Weller's my dad. I'm TJ," he said.

"How is your dad?" I asked, pleased to be able to be polite back. Mr. TJ's dad, Mr. Travis Weller, has something wrong with his legs and back, and had been in the hospital recently.

"Better, thanks," he said. "He's at home, sometimes comes into the office. Am I late?"

"A little," I said. "They're waiting for you."

He went in. I let Sloop ride his trike a bit more, but a norther'd come in over the weekend and turned the weather, so it was getting chilly already and I made him go in before it was all the way dark. We played with his stuffed animals awhile, and then I ran his bath.

"Don't forget my doughnut!" he shouted as I closed the door on him.

"I won't," I answered, through the door. "Don't you forget your ears." I went to the kitchenette, where there weren't any doughnuts. We'd forgotten to save any out for us.

Sloop would be impossible if he didn't get his doughnut. I'd have to go to the party room and hope the grown-ups hadn't eaten them all. Mom's office opens into our living room on one side and the party room on the other, so I walked through.

The leftover doughnuts were on the counter of the party room kitchenette. The tenants sat in the folding chairs, facing the counter, and Mom stood to one side. Mr. TJ walked up and down the room with an ashtray in one hand and one of those long brown cigarettes called cigarillos in the other. I pointed at the doughnuts, and Mom nodded, so I came the rest of the way in and picked up a napkin.

"Something needs to be done," Mr. Barracotta was saying. "The place is a firetrap."

"Oh, I think that's too strong a term," said Mr. TJ. "It's true that it would be easy to set on fire, but it won't go up spontaneously." He laid his cigarillo in the ashtray and set it on the edge of the counter so he could take his handkerchief out of his pocket and wipe his nose. "I won't say you don't have a right to be worried about having an abandoned house on your doorstep, after what happened down the street."

They were talking about the Brick House! I pretended to have trouble deciding between powdered and glazed doughnuts.

"Wasn't that your house, too?" asked Domie.

Mr. TJ sneezed, smiled, and nodded, moving away from the counter. "We were lucky on that one. It wasn't a large property, no one was hurt, and insurance will cover the loss. I won't pretend I don't worry about it happening again, especially since the fire marshal doesn't hold out much hope for catching the arsonists."

Marshall leaned over and said something into his mom's ear. She smiled with half her mouth, frowned with the other half, and motioned for him to be quiet.

"What does our firefighter think?" asked Domie.

Everybody looked at Mr. Sanchez. He spread his hands and shrugged his shoulders. "What am I supposed to say? Sure, somebody could torch the Brick House. But lots of buildings around here would burn better and be easier to get at. It's not only fenced, padlocked, and boarded, it's right by a bus stop. I'd think it'd be too big a risk for an arsonist to mess with, which means it's not much of a risk for us."

"But why should we have to put up with any risk at all?" asked Cheryl's mom. "Why not just tear it down, if you're not going to do anything with it?"

Tear down the Brick House! I held my breath.

"Mr. TJ, clear on the other side of the room by now, took out another cigarillo. "You'd be amazed how many restrictions there are in this town as to how a man can deal with his own property. The Little Old

Ladies in Tennis Shoes have decided that heap of brick has historical value."

I breathed again and got a noseful of smoke from his first cigarillo. I leaned over and smashed it out in the ashtray. It was still plenty long, even after squashing. I guess he'd been so busy talking and taking care of his cold he'd forgotten that he'd barely started smoking it.

"Don't ask my why," he went on. "Nobody I ever heard of ever slept there. But we have to go through all kinds of legal crud before we can take a wrecking ball to it."

I felt small and tight inside.

"Why bother, then?" asked Mom. "Why not turn it into a rec center? It's a good house, plenty of room. We could all use a place to send the kids besides that sand heap out back."

Yeah for Mom! A murmur went through the room, and a lot of people nodded, but Mr. TJ shook his head sadly. "That house is pushing ninety years old," he said. "Its wiring is old, its plumbing is ancient, we don't know what the roof's like—it could take a massive amount of capital. I'm sure I don't have to explain the state of the economy to you—"

"How much capital?" asked Mrs. Barracotta.

Mr. TJ smoked his cigarillo and blew smoke out thoughtfully. "It's hard to say."

"Couldn't you find out?" asked Cheryl's mom.

"Sure," said Mr. TJ. "It never hurts to take estimates. But don't get your hopes up."

"Mary Jane!" Sloop hollered—not very loud, yet. I scooped up the doughnuts and left, thinking about what I'd overheard while we ate and looked at TV and while I watched Sloop brush his teeth and get into bed. I did my homework at the kitchen table, and when Mom and Dad came in I asked, "What's capital?"

"Money," said Dad. "Specifically, the amount of money you need up front to do something. It's something business people are always worrying about— whether what they put their capital in will make enough money to pay them back."

"Would a rec center pay much money back?" I asked.

"No." Mom sighed. "It'll count as an improvement, and they'll have to pay more taxes on it, and it won't bring in any money unless he charges us to use it. I knew when I brought the matter up that TJ wouldn't go for it. It's just that—it would be so nice."

"He said he'd look into it," I said.

"He was being polite," said Dad. "This is the last you'll ever hear of it, I'm afraid."

"Oh." I said. They turned on the TV and sat on the couch with their backs to the armrests and their legs mixed up together. I tried to work another math problem, but I couldn't concentrate. If the Brick House got turned into a rec center, that'd be okay; it wouldn't be our private place anymore, but we could still use it. But if it got torn down, that'd be the end of it. "Who are the Little Old Ladies in Tennis Shoes that said the Brick House is historical?" I asked during a commercial.

"The Conservation Society," said Dad. "They're not all little old ladies; that's just a way of talking. They're mostly responsible for the city guidelines about what is and isn't of historical interest. If a house meets those guidelines, it practically has to be condemned before you can tear it down."

That was okay, then. The Brick House wasn't anywhere near being condemned. I took my homework on back to my room to finish up in a hurry, so I'd have a little time to look at TV or read before I went to bed.

CHAPTER SIX
Matches

THE NEXT DAY AT SCHOOL, WHILE EVERYBODY else was talking about the adobe burning, and some people about Dahomey Jackson being missing, the Brick House Burglars talked about the tenants' meeting. We agreed that the best thing that could happen would be nothing, but if the Wellers decided to tear our house down, we would fight. "We could get petitions signed and go to the Conservation Society, and—I don't know. There must be lots of stuff," said Heather.

"We could make a human wall," said Rainbow, "and block the bulldozers from coming in!"

"We don't have enough people to make a wall, silly," said Donnavita. "Besides, they won't do bulldozers to start off with. They'll use wrecking balls."

"A sit-in, then," continued Rainbow. "Domie and

Petal'd show us how." Petal is Rainbow's grand-mother. Weird names run in that family.

"Domie and Petal are stuck in the sixties," said Heather. "Nobody does sit-ins anymore."

"That doesn't mean they wouldn't work," I said. "Nobody'd knock down a house with four little girls in it."

"No," said Donnavita. "They'd carry us out first."

"So we chain ourselves to the stair rail," said Rainbow.

We talked on and on like that, getting more and more interested, until we almost wished the Wellers would decide to knock the Brick House down so we could do all these exciting things. When we got off the bus in the afternoon, though, we were glad to see it standing there, waiting for us.

"Look," I said, as a BMW pulled out of the side street. "There's Mr. TJ." We waved, and he waved back. "I wonder what he wanted."

"Maybe he forgot something," said Donnavita.

"Maybe he came to look at the house," said Heather. "There's Marshall. He might know."

Marshall was hanging around the driveway, looking discontented. "I don't know," he said, crossly, when we asked him. "He went in the house."

"Which house?" asked Donnavita. "This brick one?"

"Yes! This brick house! Which house d'you think?"

"What's the matter with you?" asked Heather.

"Nothing!" said Marshall. "I got to go to the store."

So he stomped off. Nobody else was around, so we hurried to put our books up and meet back at the

Brick House. We were getting real good at getting inside. I had a watch that shows seconds if you press the right button, so I tried to time us; but the button was too hard to hold down. "What's the matter with her?" Rainbow was saying when I got in.

She was putting out the cat food, the kittens crowding around her, and Isis was acting strange. She cried, lashed her tail, ran up to Rainbow, pawed at her leg, ran toward the door to the hall, yowled, and came back. "That's the closest she's ever come to me," said Rainbow. "Maybe she's getting used to us. Here, Isis! Nice kitty!"

"Me-rowr!" said Isis, running to the door with her body low to the ground.

"Maybe she wants us to follow her," said Donnavita, walking toward the door.

Isis yowled some more and ran a few steps into the hall, then stopped and looked back. We followed, Rainbow last because she was finishing feeding the kittens. Isis ran a few steps down the stairs.

"Do you smell something?" asked Heather.

We all sniffed. I had just been smelling the stuff last night, so I recognized it first. "Tobacco smoke," I said. "Mr. TJ must've been smoking his cigarillos in here today."

"It's all right, Isis," said Donnavita. "He's gone. He won't hurt you, or your babies."

"Meow!" cried Isis, running straight down the stairs.

We followed her, not thinking there was anything

we could do for her. This was the first time she'd treated us like anything but two-footed giants. We didn't like to let her down and spoil our chances of her being friendly. At the foot of the stairs, where the only light came through the little window above the door (that's called a transom), Isis nipped around the corner, down the hall. Heather followed, and squeaked, "Oh, crud!"

"What!" we all shouted, clattering after her; but Heather was too busy stomping on something to answer. When I got into the hall she was standing in front of the open closet with something in her hand—it was too dark to tell what. "What is it?" asked Donnavita as we clustered around.

Heather held her hand open flat. "Lookit," she said, in a small voice.

"How?" I asked. "It's dark." But my eyes were adjusting. "Matches. Mr. TJ must've dropped them."

"No, look. There's more." She held the matches closer to our faces and pointed to something sticking out the side. "I found them just like this. Only the cigarillo was lit."

"Why is there a cigarette shoved through the matchbook like that?" asked Donnavita.

The matchbook was one of those cardboard things, with the matches you tear off and a flap to tuck under the strip of black paper where you strike them. The flap was closed, with a cigarillo stuck crosswise inside, up top, where the match heads are. The cigarette had burned down to the edge of the cardboard. "This is a full book, y'all," said Heather. "If I hadn't stomped it out when I did, the cigarette would've lit all the matches."

In the closet, Rainbow ruffled through a pile of old newspapers. A spray can fell on the floor with a ringing clatter, scaring Isis even further away. "Where'd all this trash come from?" asked Rainbow. "It wasn't here before."

"The matchbook was right in the door here," said Heather, squatting down and showing us. "All this junk would've caught fire if we'd got here five minutes later. Maybe less."

Suddenly I felt as sick as she sounded. "And the house would've caught fire," I said.

"Just like that place by the school," said Heather, rolling the spray can with her foot.

"Only with us in it," said Donnavita.

"And the kittens," said Rainbow.

"Meow!" said Isis.

CHAPTER SEVEN

Detectives

WHEN WE GOT UPSTAIRS, INTO THE LIGHT, WE opened the matchbook carefully. Though the matches were the cheap kind you get at the grocery store, the cigarette was not. "That's a cigarillo," I said. "The kind Mr. TJ smokes."

The other Burglars looked at me. "And he was here this afternoon!" said Donnavita, eagerly.

"Don't be silly," I said. "Of course it wasn't Mr. TJ."

"Why not?" asked Rainbow. "Because he wears nice suits?"

Isis had settled down some and was washing Bib like there was no tomorrow. I had the minutes book open, but it wasn't any fun, taking notes, with that book of matches staring at me from the middle of the floor.

"It doesn't make any sense," I said. "Where'd all that trash come from? Somebody'd've noticed a sharp dresser like Mr. TJ hauling trash into this house."

"But it's his cigarillo," said Heather. "I've never seen anybody else smoke a brown cigarette. That proves it."

"No, it doesn't," I said, remembering. "He left half of one in the ashtray in the party room. I know because I went there to get doughnuts for Sloop, and I put it out. He was already smoking another one. Anybody could've taken it."

"Anybody in the apartments," said Heather.

We were all quiet for a minute, thinking. It could hardly be anybody from outside the apartments; why would a nontenant come into the party room? Boots crept up on the matchbook and pounced on it; but Rainbow took it away from her and hand wrestled her instead. Kittens are real cute, wrestling hands; but it was hard to pay attention to that.

"One of the grown-ups," I said. "They were all there last night except Mrs. Losoya, and they saw him put it down."

"Only it's not a grown-up thing to do, is it?" said Donnavita. "I mean, a kid might see a cigarillo sitting there and get an idea of how to make a . . . a fuse out of it, but a grown-up'd just buy his own."

"Unless he wanted to throw the blame on Mr. TJ," suggested Rainbow.

Heather shook her head. "If this'd worked, there wouldn't've been anything left of the cigarillo but a little ash at the bottom of a lot of ash. Besides, who knew Mr. TJ would walk off and leave one? It has to be somebody who just got the idea when he saw the cigarillo sitting in the ashtray."

"So what kids were there last night?" asked Donnavita.

"None," I said. "Just me. And a baby. And Marshall—I guess he counts. But he wouldn't do this."

Heather didn't say anything.

"Neither—neither would Roxanne," said Donnavita. "She went over there when the meeting was breaking up, because she wanted to ask Mr. Sanchez something about her fire-safety class."

"Just about anybody could've wandered through," said Rainbow. Sunshine pounced on Boots's tail, so that she left off fighting Rainbow's hand and pounced back. "We can't prove anything this way. What kind of person would try to burn down the Brick House?"

"Somebody who likes to watch things burn," said Heather. She didn't sound like herself at all; kind of flat.

"A pyromaniac," said Donnavita. "Or somebody who wants—I don't know. We can't figure it out this way. It could be somebody who looks mega-normal."

"It could be Los Red Dukes," said Rainbow. Donnavita and Heather both brightened up again at that suggestion; but I didn't think it was right.

"It's the sort of thing gangs do," I said, "but that doesn't prove anything. Jimmy wasn't at the meeting, and we haven't seen any of the gang hanging around today."

"They burned that other place," said Donnavita quickly.

"We think they did, but nobody saw them. And that was a different kind of fire—I mean, this would've been a daytime fire, and that was in the middle of the night. Why would they do it different?"

"Because Jimmy's mother lives close enough to get burned up if it spreads," said Rainbow. "At night she's, you know . . ."

We did. We all know what cheap wine smells like because we all know Mrs. Losoya. Mom and Dad say it's sad, and it is; but it's also pretty disgusting. All day she's kind of wobbly and doesn't speak well; at night she's either in a really bad mood and yells at anybody who gets near her (mostly Jimmy), or dead asleep. She'd be hard to save from a fire at night. You'd either have to fight her or carry her.

Mom and Dad hadn't said anything about Jimmy showing up at the meeting. Anyway, he wouldn't have had to get the cigarillo during the meeting. The lock on that door isn't much good (I think Mom complained about that to Mr. TJ at the meeting, too; she usually does), and I know for a fact that Jimmy gets in there sometimes when it's locked. For a long while his mom's refrigerator wasn't working right, so he'd break in to get ice out of the one in the party room. When Mom complained about it, Jimmy (at least, we're sure it was him) tore down the curtains, wrote dirty words in Magic Marker all over, stuffed an old pair of undershorts in the sink drain, and left the water running. By the time we got back from the movie we'd gone to that night, the place was flooded. That was way back last year, about the time Mr. Travis Weller went to the hospital, but the lock still hasn't been changed.

But why should he break in last night?

"There's no point us straining our brains," I said. "Let's give the matchbook to Mr. Sanchez. He'll know what to do."

"No!" said Heather and Donnavita, both together, so loudly the kittens and Isis jumped.

"Are you crazy?" asked Rainbow. "He'd tell our folks. They'd tell Mr. TJ, he'd board up that window, and we and Isis both couldn't get in anymore."

"Somebody might even say we did it," said Donnavita.

"We'd get skinned alive," said Heather.

"That's better than burned alive, isn't it?" I pointed out.

"We won't get burned alive. If it's just some kid playing around, they probably won't try again."

"What if it's a pyromaniac?"

"I move," said Donnavita, "that every day the first item of business, even before we feed the kittens, is to check the house for fires."

"There's a fire extinguisher stuck way in the back under our kitchen sink," said Heather. "I'll bring it tomorrow. Second the motion. All in favor say aye."

"Aye," said Rainbow.

"Aye," I said, "but I still want to tell Mr. Sanchez."

"We'll have to be detectives," said Heather. "Whoever set that fire, we have to find them and stop them."

"How?" I asked, crossly. "What are we going to do to them?"

"We'll call in the grown-ups if it's somebody like Los Red Dukes," said Heather, "but if it's some kid, we won't. It wouldn't be right."

"Why wouldn't it? All they'd get is fire-safety classes, like Roxanne."

"We'll decide when we catch her," said Donnavita. "Okay?"

"You mean if," I said. "We don't know anything about catching arsonists."

"Maybe whoever it is won't try it again," said Rainbow. "C'mon, Mary Jane; it'd be stupid to tell Mr. Sanchez and then never have the arsonist come back. We'd've given up the Brick House for nothing."

That was a point. Not a good enough one, though. "Why shouldn't they come back? I move—"

"What for? You know you're outvoted," said Heather.

"I want a vote for the record," I said, writing furiously. "When we get caught, I'll show this around so everybody knows it wasn't me that wouldn't go to the authorities."

So we voted on turning the matchbook over to Mr. Sanchez, three nays to one aye; then we decided to put the matchbook in the window seat with the rest of our stuff, only we were going to need a box to keep it safe. We had been going to play with Donnavita's model case, trying out the makeup and stuff. She had an old broken camera we'd meant to do a fashion shoot with. We didn't feel like it anymore, though, so we closed the meeting.

Everything was happening at once again because it was that same evening the fire marshals came.

They knocked while I was wiping counters and Dad was rinsing dishes. Mom let in two men and turned the TV off. "Hey!" said Sloop.

"It's not polite to run the TV while there's company," said Mom. "You can play in your room for a while."

"There's nothing to do in my room," said Sloop.

"There's lots of stuff to do," said Mom, "more than there is out here. Daddy and Mary Jane and I have to talk to these men, and it's not stuff you're interested in."

I didn't know who they were yet, but I liked being included with the grown-ups, so I said, "You can borrow my Barbie car as long as they stay, Sloop," and he went for that. He's got his own cars, but he keeps jamming the wheels. So we got him out of the way, and Mom said, "This is Mr. Halliday and Mr. Wyclaviak." (I know that's the right spelling because I asked him.) "They're from the fire marshal's office."

Suddenly I didn't feel so good about being included with the grown-ups anymore.

It turned out they were mostly interested in Los Red

Dukes. Luckily they didn't ask me any questions I would've had to tell a straight-out lie to. I was surprised how little they knew about Los Red Dukes. They knew there was a gang around the adobe house that night of the fire because of the graffiti. Mr. TJ had told them he thought one of the gang members might live in these apartments, so they'd come here, figuring Mom being apartment manager would know.

I could tell she wasn't comfortable with the idea of ratting on her neighbors. "Well," she said, "there is one teenage boy here who's a little wild." She explained about the party room. They looked mildly interested, and asked twice if we were sure there'd been no attempt to set anything on fire.

"And was the boy disciplined after that?" asked Mr. Halliday.

Mom and Dad looked at each other. "I cornered him and gave him a talking-to," said Dad. "And we fixed his refrigerator."

"But you didn't confront his parents?"

"Isabel's not the sort of woman it does any good to confront," said Mom. "You'll understand when you talk to her."

Mr. Wyclaviak made a note on a pad. "I see. Is there anything more recent than this?"

Mom and Dad looked at each other again. Normally I wouldn't have felt right ratting, either, but if Jimmy was going around burning down buildings—especially if he planned to burn down the Brick House—I had no sympathy for him. "Oh, come on," I said. "We all know he started Los Red Dukes. He's the leader."

"You know that for a fact, young lady?" asked Mr. Halliday.

Mostly when somebody calls me "young lady" it means I'm in trouble, but I liked the way Mr. Halliday said it. "Sure," I said. "Everybody knows it. When they're not doing gang stuff, they hang out in the parking lot."

"And this Jimmy Losoya is the leader?"

I nodded. "He's always the first to do things. And Roxanne goes to his school. Everybody there knows about it."

Then they had to find out who Roxanne was, and who else might know stuff about Jimmy. I told them to ask Rainbow. I had to tell all about what Los Red Dukes did in the parking lot, which wasn't a whole heck of a lot, and none of it except smoking having to do with fire, which is what they wanted to know about. When I told about how they'd ridden their motorbikes at us, though, I remembered something small. "It looked like Jimmy was riding straight for me," I said, "and I'd been saying a jump rope rhyme about setting fires. Maybe he had a guilty conscience and it ticked him off."

"Maybe," said Mr. Halliday, "but it's not evidence."

After they'd found out what all I knew, they took down the apartment numbers for the Losoyas, Roxanne, and Rainbow. "I doubt it'll do you any good to talk to Jimmy or Isabel, either one," said Mom. "Isabel won't even admit Jimmy's in a gang, and by this hour she's probably asleep or incoherent."

"We've got to try, ma'am," said Mr. Wyclaviak. "If y'all see or think of anything that might be helpful, let us know. And don't get it too set in your heads that the gang's responsible. People set fires for fun and profit all the time." He looked straight at me. "You'd be doing nobody any favors by not telling on them. Lots of arsonists die in their own fires."

"Yes, sir," I said. For a minute I thought/hoped/feared he would ask me to promise to call the fire department with any sign of arson I found, but they said good night and went on.

A few minutes later we heard screaming in Spanish. They were trying to talk to Mrs. Losoya; and it wasn't working.

I went and rescued my Barbie car from Sloop. He swore up and down he hadn't done anything to make the front axle come off, but it had anyway. Dad fixed it, but it never has rolled as well since. Little brothers are such a pain.

CHAPTER EIGHT

Jobs

RAINBOW AND ROXANNE BOTH WERE MAD AT ME
next morning. "What did you want to sic the fire marshals on me for?" asked Roxanne. "I don't know any
more about Jimmy than anybody else."

"You're the one that goes to school with him," I said.

"So what? If I knew anything about him setting that
fire, I'd've gone straight to Mr. Sanchez." She tossed
her head so her hair flew around. "Why does everybody
come to me when somebody else does something stupid? Dahomey Jackson's dad came around yesterday
asking me about why she disappeared—how'm I supposed to know? And now Jimmy!"

Donnavita said nothing, just looked at Roxanne
sideways.

"And what made you think I'd rat on anybody?" demanded Rainbow. "Domie says, any time you bring the police in, you make things worse." She peered down the street to see if the bus was coming. "Mrs. Losoya was up all night banging things around. She and Jimmy had a big fight at midnight. If I fall asleep in school, it's your fault."

"Is not," I said. "They wake you up with their fights all the time, whether the marshals've been to see them or not."

"If you'd send them to Mrs. Losoya, I'm surprised you didn't send them to Marshall," said Heather. "He was at the fire."

"They were asking more about Jimmy than the fire," I said. "Anyway, what could Marshall tell them?"

"He'd've been thrilled to have them ask, though," said Roxanne. "What was that joke he made at the meeting, Heather?"

"I don't know what you mean," said Heather.

"Mr. Sanchez heard him say something to your mom about, if he was at a fire, he'd be a fire marshal. I thought that was pretty clever, for somebody with 'problems.' "

"That's our bus," said Heather.

Roxanne goes in the other direction, so we left her standing on the curb. We sat all together in the sideways seats at the front, which you're supposed to give up to old and handicapped people if any get on. "What's bugging you?" I asked Donnavita.

"Oh, nothing." She sighed.

"Right," said Heather. "You're chewing your fingernails and rolling your eyes at Roxanne for the fun of it."

"I am not chewing my fingernails!" Donnavita took her hand away from her mouth. "I've got a hangnail and I don't have any clippers, that's all." She used to chew her nails something awful, but she's mostly broken herself of it, because you can't be a model with raggedy fingernails.

"So what's Roxanne done this time?" asked Rainbow.

"Nothing, really." Donnavita's hand started to go to her mouth again, but she caught it and laid it down flat on her history book. "She's just getting megagoopy about Mr. Sanchez. She's writing all over her notebook—Mrs. Herbert Sanchez, Mrs. H. Sanchez, Roxanne Barracotta-Sanchez—it's dumb."

"His first name is Herbert?" I asked. He must've been an ugly baby, to get stuck with a name like that.

"But so what?" asked Rainbow. "You don't have to look in her notebook."

"She talks about him all the time, too. All about how exciting and noble being a firefighter is. I get sick of it." She picked at the hangnail till it tore off. (I've done this myself, and it's a bad idea. You wind up with another hangnail further down your finger.) "She thinks it'd be so romantic, to watch him fight a fire. I bet she wouldn't be a bit sorry to see the Brick House burn down, if she got to see Mr. Sanchez putting it out."

"That's pretty dumb, even for Roxanne," I said.

"Firefighters get killed and hurt all the time. Don't they teach her that in the fire-safety class?"

"Probably," said Donnavita. "But she only ever learns stuff she wants to know. Once she passes a test, everything on it that she doesn't care about gets lost. At least that's what she says when I want help with my homework."

None of us was much good in school that day. I started a list of clues to the arsonist in the back of my science notebook, but they didn't amount to much. Jimmy Losoya was a good suspect for the adobe building, but a lousy one for the Brick House. He wouldn't have any reason to take the cigarillo from the party room, even if he'd come in for some reason and seen it. (I'd forgotten to ask Mom and Dad what kids had come by while the party room was open. I wrote a note to myself to do that tonight.) Jimmy buys his own cigarettes all the time, even though he's not old enough. Maybe he bought cigarillos to use in arson because they are longer than ordinary cigarettes, and would give him more time to get away before the fire started? I wrote it down as a possibility, but we hadn't seen him anywhere near the Brick House yesterday afternoon.

It took us a while to get into the Brick House that day. Marshall was hanging around again (his school starts and gets out earlier than ours), and when Rainbow went to put up her books and sweater Mrs. Losoya came out to yell at her. We all heard her from inside our apartments and ran out, us and Mom and Ms. Sonntag (that's Heather's mom) and Roxanne. Domie and Petal didn't come out because they were both at work.

Mrs. Losoya was in her robe and tennis shoes, with her hair sticking up all over the place, yelling, "My boy he don't start no fires, not never no more! What you want to get my boy in trouble for?" Then she went off in a long string of Spanish.

Rainbow looked smaller even than usual. "But I—ma'am, listen—I didn't tell anybody anything—"

"You leave her alone!" shouted Marshall; but Mom hurried around him to sweep Mrs. Losoya into her apartment.

"Mi chico no es en el gang!" shouted Mrs. Losoya as Mom went in with her and shut the door.

Rainbow was shaking all over. "It's not fair!" she said. "She should've been yelling at Mary Jane!"

"She probably would've if she'd seen Mary Jane first," said Ms. Sonntag. "You've got to realize, Mrs. Losoya's not thinking—she's reacting to whatever happens to be close to her."

It took forever for things to settle down after that. Ms. Sonntag and Roxanne, and Mom after she got Mrs. Losoya quiet and came out, and even Marshall, stood around saying the same things over and over, while we kept looking at the Brick House, expecting to see it explode or something. Rainbow wasn't upset nearly as long as Mom and Ms. Sonntag.

Finally Heather distracted them by asking Mom if we could borrow the backpack again, and asking her mom if we could have cookies for mountaineering provisions. They both said yes. I brought the pack over to Heather's apartment and we put the fire extinguisher in the bottom, the cat stuff in the middle, and a bag of Chips Ahoy on top.

The parking lot still wasn't empty—Mr. Sanchez and Mr. Anstruther were unloading groceries, and Roxanne was helping—so we played mountaineers for real till the coast was clear.

Then we grabbed our chance and dashed across the lot, over the fence, and up the side of the house in what was probably record time but I didn't think to time it. The kittens were real glad to see Rainbow, and she fed them while the rest of us searched the house, finding no fires anywhere.

We opened the meeting, sitting in a circle by the mattress and eating cookies. Old business was how to detect the arsonist. "We don't know what we're doing, y'all," I said, bringing out my list of people and evidence. "This is the best I could do."

They passed it around and looked it over.

"This is pathetic," said Heather, pointing to the "Suspects" list. "How can you possibly call Marshall a suspect?"

"And Roxanne?" demanded Donnavita.

"I don't," I said. "Marshall and Mr. TJ are the only people we know for sure were hanging around the

Brick House that day. Except for us, and we know we didn't do it. And Roxanne could've got hold of a cigarillo, so I put her down."

"We don't even know for sure it came from the ashtray in the party room," said Rainbow. "It probably didn't. They'd all be smoked short, and the one in the matchbook was pretty long."

"One of them wasn't smoked hardly at all," I said, and reminded them about the one I'd put out. "Even the ones he finished he didn't smoke real short."

Donnavita made a face. "It's a shame we can't find out whether it was one of those or not. If we knew it wasn't, we could take Roxanne off the list, and we'd know—I don't know—more than we do now."

"We don't even know what we need to know," I said. "I mean, if we were fire marshals, what would we be looking for?"

"I can find that out," said Donnavita. "Roxanne's got this workbook for the fire-safety class. If it doesn't say there, I can ask her, and if she doesn't know, she can ask in class."

"All right," said Heather. "But only if you can ask her some way that doesn't make her wonder. Remember this is top secret!" She frowned at me. "We shouldn't even put it in the minutes book."

I'd been forgetting to write, but I remembered now. "We should too," I said. "What if we get too close to the truth and the arsonist kidnaps us? The minutes book will be the only clue to what happened to us."

"If anybody can find it," said Donnavita.

"Arsonists don't kidnap people, kidnappers do," said Heather.

"Who says you can't be both?" asked Rainbow.

Heather tossed her head, as if she were getting her hair out of her eyes, even though her hair was all brushed back from her forehead. "Anyway," she said, "Donnavita shouldn't be doing all the work. We should all have jobs. Mary Jane, you see if you can get information out of your mom."

"Information about what?" I asked.

"About where that cigarillo went, for one thing. If she remembers dumping a long one out, that lets out the people at the meeting. If she doesn't, you'll have to find out who was at the meeting, especially what kids and teenagers showed up."

"What am I supposed to say—'Hey, Mom, I'm real interested in ashtrays this week'?"

"You'll think of something," said Heather.

"Oh! You know what!" Rainbow had worked her shoelace out of her shoe and was wiggling it across the floor for Sunshine and Nyota to pounce on. She looked up at me and forgot to wiggle for a minute, struck by this idea. "Your mom might be a witness!"

"A witness to what?" I asked. "She's inside all day."

"Not all day! She comes out when Sloop wants to play outside and there's nobody to watch him, and she goes to the apartments to look at leaks and things, and . . . and she can look out the window. Mr. TJ probably came in to talk to her. She can tell us who besides him and Marshall were hanging around!"

"Why not ask Marshall?" I asked. "We know he was outside."

"Okay. That'll be my job," said Heather.

"What about me?" asked Rainbow.

"What about you?" asked Heather.

"What's my job?"

We were all quiet for a minute. I knew what her job should be. Only I wasn't going to tell her to do it.

"Somebody ought to check up on Jimmy," said Donnavita, and then added hastily, "but the fire marshals are doing that. You don't have to do anything, Rainbow."

"I do too," said Rainbow. "You can't be vice president and not do anything."

"You can too," I said. "That's what vice presidents are for. They wait around till the president can't do her job, and then they're all set to do it in place of her."

Rainbow's mouth made a straight line. "Is that why I'm vice president? 'Cause y'all don't think I can do anything?"

"No!" said Heather, scornfully. "You've got a job. You're chief representative to the cats. That's just as important as detecting the arsonist, you know. If it weren't for the cats, this club couldn't exist. And kittens are more important than buildings, because they're alive." She was talking a little fast now, not giving Rainbow a chance to say anything. "In fact, I move that as the next order of business we take these bowls out and wash them. They're getting kind of icky."

"And I need to collect dues," said Donnavita, "so we can get some real cat food."

"And flea powder," I said, scratching my arm. "The mattress is swarming with them."

That changed the subject, and we played with the kittens the rest of the meeting. But the right word for the way Rainbow looked is *grim*.

CHAPTER NINE
Suspicions

ANYBODY WHO THINKS IT'S EASY TO PUMP THEIR mothers for information about what she emptied out of ashtrays three or four days ago, without arousing her curiosity, is welcome to try it. I about beat my brains to death all day, trying to think of some way even to bring the subject up. I was doing my homework before inspiration struck.

I helped her put Sloop to bed and then, before she could go back to the TV, I asked, "Mom, what's the biggest part of cleaning up after a meeting?"

"The biggest part?" You know how grown-ups repeat things to give themselves time to think when you ask them something totally off the wall. "The refreshments, I guess. You've got to put them up right away, or you'll draw bugs."

"And you put off the rest of it, like emptying the ashtrays and stuff?" If she'd let the ashtrays sit overnight, it'd give the arsonist more time to find the long cigarillo.

"Yes, the rest of it waits till morning." She looked at me funny while she got out milk and cheese for a bedtime snack.

I hurried on. "And when you emptied the ashtrays at the meeting the other night, were they more full or less full than when you first started being apartment manager?"

"Honey, what on earth are you talking about?" she asked.

"My history teacher likes to give us extra credit paragraphs," I said, which was true. "Explain how something happens and give specific examples." That was also true. "So, explain how something's changed over the last five years." She hadn't asked anything like that, but it's the sort of question she does ask. "So I thought if meetings changed, or . . . or if maybe people are smoking less now than they were, that would be the kind of thing she likes us to cover. Everyday stuff." And it's true; that history teacher's real big on how people lived, instead of just how they voted and what battles they fought. Donnavita says it's harder, but I say it's more interesting.

Anyway, Mom bought it. She put the cheese onto a plate and poured out milk and said, "Tenants' meetings don't change very fast. We still serve coffee and doughnuts and people still complain about the water pressure in the showers. It's funny you should ask about the smoking, though. When I first took this job, most people weren't smoking at meetings, but the ones that did smoked nasty, cheap cigarettes down to the filter. Most of what I cleaned out on Monday morning were those expensive cigarillos, and they hadn't been smoked very short."

"That's not a fair comparison, though," said Dad, coming into the kitchenette and getting the crackers off the top of the refrigerator. "That good ole boy who smoked like a chimney moved out years ago, and TJ was at this last meeting with his fancy smokes. His father never smokes anything but a pipe, and he only does it in the open air."

"That's so," said Mom. "Travis Weller's a real gentleman."

"And TJ's a fake one." Dad laughed.

"He is not," I said. "He remembers my name and everything."

"That's a good sign," said Dad, "but you've got to look at everything a person does. A lot of what TJ does is flash, done to impress people. Take those cigarillos. They cost more per pack than steak costs per pound. And what does he do with them? Lights one, waves it around, smokes it halfway, and then walks off and leaves it while he lights another. I don't think he picks them because he likes the taste, any more than he picked out that BMW because he liked the color. He wants everybody to see that he doesn't have to worry about what things cost."

This was too good a chance to pass up, even if it

did mean joining Dad in criticizing Mr. TJ. "He does waste a lot of those cigarillos," I admitted.

We sat around the table eating cheese and crackers, the TV running in the background. Mom said, "Anyway, this won't help you with your paragraph."

"What about something else, then?" I couldn't believe how well this was going. "Do more people show up at tenants' meetings, or do maybe more kids come, or what?"

Mom shrugged. "Everybody but Isabel showed up this last time, because we were all concerned about that fire, but that was unusual. And kids don't hardly show up at all, never did. There was you, and a few of the babies, and Marshall. He's started coming to prove he's grown-up enough to take an interest."

"And Roxanne wandered in toward the end," said Dad, breaking a slice of cheese in half to split it between two crackers, "because she'd thought of an excuse to drool on Sanchez. That's about how things go. You'd better forget about the meetings."

"I think five years is too small a time span," said Mom. "She should have asked you for changes during your lifetime. That'd be easy."

That was all I could find out about what I needed to know, because she and Dad started talking about what had and hadn't changed, and what was better, and what was worse, and what was just different. Dad decided I should write my paragraph on international communism, and Mom thought that was too obvious, that I'd get a better grade if I wrote about something fewer people'd think of, like TV continuity. (Continuity is how much stuff continues from episode to episode; like whether a problem gets solved and forgotten in half an hour or if they only solve part of it and it comes back next week or next month.) If I'd really had that topic for extra credit, I could've gotten an A.

I thought I'd done okay pumping Mom, but next morning on the bus the other Burglars didn't think much of my results. "I don't see where we know anything more than we used to," said Heather. "We already knew pretty much who was at the meeting, and you didn't even ask her about who was around the Brick House right before we got home."

"Give me a break," I complained. "It about busted my head open getting the answers I did. Anyway, you were supposed to be asking Marshall who was around."

"I did." Heather turned to Donnavita. "Did you know Roxanne ditched school that day?"

"She wouldn't!" Donnavita looked surprised and— scared?

"She did!" Heather nodded firmly. "Marshall saw her get off the bus a little after he did. Mr. TJ was already in the house and"—she leaned toward Donnavita— "the door and gate were wide open! Anybody could have gone in, even while Mr. TJ was there!"

"But—that'd be dumb—" began Rainbow.

Donnavita was mad. "You saying Roxanne did it?"

"You said yourself she wouldn't care if the Brick House burned down, as long as she got to watch Mr. Sanchez at a fire."

I couldn't believe Heather was being this mean. "She didn't mean it," I said. "C'mon, Heather, what's the matter with you?"

"You might as well say it could've been Marshall," said Donnavita spitefully. "He was there, too."

After that, Rainbow and I couldn't do anything with them. They fought all the way to school, and by the time the bus stopped they were swearing not to speak to each other ever again. They wouldn't eat at the same table and Rainbow and I decided if we ate with either of them, it'd make things worse, so we sat with the history teacher. By the end of the day, we were pretty ticked off ourselves. We had to all go home on the same bus and get off at the same stop, but I don't think we would've had a Burglars meeting at all if Marshall hadn't waited for us at the bus stop.

"Hey, Heather!" he said, and he didn't sound any too happy with her. "I'll prove it to you!"

Heather turned pink. "I believe you, okay?" she muttered.

"Believe what?" I asked Heather.

"Prove what?" Rainbow asked Marshall.

Heather hurried to the side street and the rest of us followed, Donnavita looking meanly interested. Marshall talked to us because Heather was so far ahead. "She thinks I'm playing with matches!" he complained. "She was asking me all kinds of questions, about fires and things. She thinks I'm dumb!" he shouted after her. "She thinks I'd set a fire right where

76

I live and little girls play and that mama cat's got her kittens! That's what she thinks!"

Heather turned around at the gate and shouted back, "I said I was sorry! But somebody did try to burn this house and you do hang around a lot and I couldn't help remembering that game you used to play with Dad's lighter! So I wondered, okay! I told you my secret and I said I was sorry and if that isn't good enough for you I don't know what I can do about it!"

"You thought Marshall—?" Donnavita goggled.

"You told him the secret?" I goggled, too.

"Will y'all chill out?" said Rainbow, standing between Heather and Marshall. "The whole world doesn't have to know about this."

"Yeah, yeah, yeah," said Heather, kicking the ground. "I'm a terrible person, all right? I admit it. Now leave me alone."

"No," said Marshall, grabbing hold of her arm. "First I'm going to show you."

"Show her what?" I asked.

"What my secret is. You make her stay right here." He handed her arm to me, like I was going to be able to keep her from running off if she wanted to. Marshall grabbed hold of the fence and went over in two steps. As soon as the gate rattled, Isis popped out from under the front porch. "Hi, Mama kitty," he said, reaching down to pet her. She rubbed against his leg.

We all goggled now. Isis'd never even let Rainbow touch her, but here she was loving up to Marshall! He petted her awhile, then reached under the porch and dragged out a can, one of those big round ones people send cookies in at Christmas. He took the lid off, and Isis meowed, rubbing between his feet as he came to show it to us. It was half-full of cat food, with a bowl stuck in it like a scoop.

"I've been feeding her," he said. "That makes her my cat. But you've got to not tell anybody, or I'll tell on y'all. Mom'd be mad if she knew I spent my lunch money on cat food, but she'd be a lot madder if she knew y'all were crawling around empty houses with fires in them."

"Why did you have to tell him that?" I asked Heather. "We all swore secrecy."

Heather made a face. "Wasn't Sloop ever smarter than you thought he was?" she asked crossly. "I was so worried about Marshall maybe being the arsonist, I didn't watch what I said and he caught me. But he won't tell!"

"And I showed you my secret." Marshall scooped the bowl full and set it down for Isis, who started eating at once. "That's fair, right?"

"Yes," said Rainbow. "I'm glad you've fed Isis."

"But it's a secret," he warned her again, putting the lid back on the can and hiding it, and the bowl (which Isis followed, protesting because she'd barely started eating) back under the porch.

"We'll keep yours if you keep ours," said Donnavita. "Heather says you saw Roxanne here the other day."

Marshall nodded, and got back over the gate the

same way he'd gotten in. "She gets out early a lot. But she's got permission. She told me."

"She's lying," said Donnavita.

"Didn't you see anybody else?" asked Rainbow.

"That man," said Marshall, "with the suitcase."

"Suitcase?" I said. "You mean briefcase?"

"Whatever. The man at the meeting. He left the door open. And I see Mary Jane's mom, and Sloop, and Jimmy all the time."

"You mean Jimmy was around when Mr. TJ had the door open?" Rainbow pounced, too fast.

You've got to be careful, talking to Marshall. He drew back. "Sometime around then," he said. "He's always around."

"I knew he was our best suspect!" said Rainbow, with satisfaction. "Did you see him go in here?"

"I don't think so." Marshall was beginning to sound confused. "You mean—Jimmy tried to burn up my mama cat?"

"We don't know yet," said Heather. "Lay off, Rainbow. We can't talk about it till we figure it out for sure."

"You tell me when you do," said Marshall. "I'll teach that Jimmy to try to burn my cat!"

For a minute I was afraid he'd get so upset he'd have a seizure, which is really scary, but Heather knows how to talk to him. "You'll be the first to know," she said. "Will you be our lookout while we go in? We've got a lot of stuff to do."

So he stood lookout instead of me, and we had our meeting after all.

CHAPTER TEN
Things Look Bad

AS SOON AS WE HAD SEARCHED THE HOUSE, FED the kittens, and fetched the minutes book from the window seat, Donnavita started the meeting by saying to Heather, "I'm sorry I was mad at you all day. If you'd just told me you were feeling bad because you'd been suspecting Marshall, I wouldn't've been."

"Yeah, well, it's not the sort of thing you like to talk about," said Heather. "I'm sorry I dragged Roxanne into it."

"But the thing that made me maddest about that was that I was afraid it might be true," said Donnavita.

I was getting my pen started, drawing circles in the corner of the page, and I stopped to stare at her.

"But—you didn't even find out till this morning that she was around," said Rainbow.

"So? She won't talk about anything but fires or anybody but Mr. Sanchez. The day before we found the matchbook, Mom and Dad were talking about making the Brick House a rec center, and she said, right out, she wished it'd burn down because it wasn't good for anything anyway." We all looked at each other. I felt like something inside me had stopped. "And then you said Marshall said she was skipping class—I'm scared." Her voice started sounding high and tight. "I don't want Roxy to be the arsonist."

"She probably isn't," said Heather. "I mean, she's never burned anything down before, has she?"

"The school bathroom."

"That was an accident," I said.

"That's what she told us and Mr. Sanchez. But what if—see, she won't tell anybody who the friend was with her, that got the dope. So I thought, maybe she really did set the fire on purpose and made up the dope story because she didn't want Mr. Sanchez to think she was worse than a murderer."

We all thought about that. "You should talk to her," said Heather. "Today. Only try to be smarter about it than I was with Marshall, okay? I wouldn't trust Roxanne to keep a secret."

Donnavita nodded.

I made circles in the air with my seven-color pen. "Look, should I be putting all this stuff about Marshall and Roxanne in the minutes? It's kind of . . . personal."

"Go ahead," said Heather. "It's like the detective says

in my mom's Agatha Christie books. You can turn up a lot of stuff you don't like, trying to find out the truth. Everything has to go in the minutes book, or we might miss a clue."

"That's not what you said yesterday," said Rainbow.

"Yesterday I was afraid I was going to have to cover for Marshall."

"Well, give me time," I said. "There's a lot to write down." So they played with the kittens while I put down everything that'd happened. It was kind of a pain, but I'm glad I got everything in, because most of this story is coming from the minutes book. I tried writing with the floor for a table, lying on my stomach, but the kittens kept walking on the book.

When I was all caught up, I said so, and asked for old business. "Did you talk to Roxanne at all?" I asked Donnavita. "Did you find out anything about how to catch an arsonist?"

"Oh, that was easy," said Donnavita, but she didn't sound too happy about it. "I just started talking about the other house that burned, and she took it from there. She may be ditching school, but she sure isn't ditching that fire-safety class! She said arsonists are hardly ever caught, because unless the firefighters get lucky all the evidence, like fingerprints, gets burned up. You almost have to have somebody see the arsonist, or prove they were the only person with a chance to do it. Like, if we saw Marshall, and Roxanne, and Jimmy, and Mr. TJ, all hanging around this house, and then it burned down, unless we actually saw

Jimmy light the match he could say it was one of the others, and they wouldn't be able to prove it wasn't."

"Bummer," said Rainbow.

Donnavita nodded. "And it doesn't take very long to start a fire, but it might take a long time for anybody to notice. If Mr. TJ came in and went upstairs, Jimmy or . . . or Roxanne could come in after him, pile the trash under the stairs, set that cigarillo fuse, and clear out. Jimmy could hop on his motorbike, or Roxanne could grab a bus, and they could be long gone before the trash caught fire. And then, if Mr. TJ or one of us didn't notice the trash, nobody'd know anything about it till the outside of the house started burning. Roxanne said her fire-safety teacher said the reason there was any evidence left of that adobe house being set on fire on purpose was that that house didn't have any glass in the windows, so the air got at the fire right away and made it burn very fast and somebody called in about it before all the trash was burned."

"Air makes fires burn faster?" asked Heather.

"Uh-huh. That's why you're supposed to cover it with a blanket if you see a fire—to smother it."

"And I guess water's to drown it," I said.

"So how come you blow matches out?" asked Rainbow.

Donnavita sighed and rolled her eyes. "How do I know? I'm just telling you what Roxanne says. The point is, unless the arsonist tries again, and we see him do it, we're not going to be able to prove anything, because Marshall remembers too many people being around when we found the matchbook. We can't catch anybody on that one."

That was discouraging. How likely were we to be in the Brick House when the arsonist tried again? "We'll just have to do the best we can," said Heather. "Maybe next time, there'll be a different set of people around, and we can narrow it down. I'll have Marshall keep his eyes open."

"I don't want there to be a next time," I said.

"That isn't even the worst part," said Donnavita.

I moaned. "I don't want to hear it."

"Tough. You've got to." But Donnavita didn't seem too eager to say it. She sat and chewed her nails till Heather shoved her knee and told her to get on with it.

"Roxanne says almost all fires happen at night. She was spouting off numbers, like between midnight and five or something. When the whole world's asleep, anyway. We may not be able to catch the next fire, because if the arsonist can figure out how to get into the Brick House without Mr. TJ leaving the door open, he may do it while we're asleep."

"No, he won't," said Rainbow. "If it's somebody who lives here, they'll want to set the fire when people can get out of the apartments in case it spreads."

"They might not figure on it spreading," said Heather. "It's built of brick. And why should it get all the way to the apartments? There's nothing but parking lot in between, and that won't burn."

"Cars burn," I said.

This was making us all sick to our stomachs, and the more we talked the less we felt like we could do anything, so we stopped and played with the kittens and did a fashion shoot with the model case. I could see why Donnavita didn't want her big sister to be the arsonist. We complain a lot about what an airhead Roxanne is, but she lets Donnavita have all her old makeup and cold cream, and shows her how to use it. And she used to tell us scary stories, all about the Donkey Lady and the Tiger Lady and the haunted railroad tracks where the school bus got hit by the train.

Eventually we all went home. Heather and I left last, and while we were waiting for Rainbow to get to the ground, she said to me, "Be sure you ask your mom about who was around that day."

"What for?" I asked. "We already know from Marshall."

"He wasn't around the whole time Mr. TJ was in the house. And he—could get confused." Seeing Rainbow dash across the yard to the fence, she climbed out onto the roof. "Inside his head, he's younger than us, you know. Sometimes he gets his days mixed up."

"I'll try," I said. "I don't know how, though."

I didn't get any brilliant ideas, but by dinnertime I'd thought of a way at least to get on the subject. After we said grace and started passing the spaghetti, I said, "I wonder what Mr. TJ found out looking at the Brick House the other day."

"He didn't look at the Brick House, dear," said Mom. "He said he would, but I guess he hasn't had time yet."

"But he was in there Monday," I said, surprised.

Mom and Dad looked at me. Sloop kept cutting his spaghetti—he likes to chop it into teeny tiny pieces with the side of his fork. "He was?" said Mom. "I never saw him."

So much for her as a witness. "Marshall did," I said.

"What was Marshall doing?" asked Dad.

"Looking for that cat," I mumbled. "And I saw a BMW drive off after we got off the bus."

"Marshall must've been confused," said Mom. "TJ never stops by without looking in on me."

"He talked about it the same day," I said. "He said the man from the meeting went in and left the door standing open."

"Well, forevermore," said Mom.

"I expect he was in a hurry," said Dad.

"I wonder what he found out, though." Mom shook grated cheese onto her spaghetti till she had a big yellow pile on top of her sauce.

"Probably not much, if he didn't bring in a roofer and an electrician. Did Marshall see anybody else?"

"Only the usual people. Jimmy, Mom, like that."

"Jimmy was around an awful lot that afternoon, I remember," said Mom. "Working on that silly motorbike all day when he should've been in school, and roaring off on it when he should have been on his way home." She mixed her spaghetti and cheese together. "I'm surprised TJ left the door open with him around."

"I doubt TJ knows him by sight," said Dad.

"But he looks like such a punk, wearing that leather

jacket even in weather like this." (After a little cold spell it was getting warmer every day.) "Well, I'll call. Probably TJ was doing a preliminary inspection on his own, and will bring the specialists out whenever he and they have time. It's not as if this were his only property, or his only worry. This is a bad time to be in the business of managing real estate, and of course it's his dad who's the real talent at Weller and Weller. It must've been hard for TJ, doing everything on his own while Travis was in the hospital."

"Not much anybody can do about Mr. Weller's legs," said Dad, "but if they hang on long enough, real estate has to get profitable again. More people get made every day, but I don't see anybody making more land."

"This is true," said Mom, "but meantime they've got to pay taxes and insurance, not to mention salaries for people like me."

"Why should they pay insurance?" I asked. "I thought insurance was something that paid out money."

"Nobody's in the business of giving away money," said Dad. "Say you agree to pay the insurance people five hundred dollars every three months or so, and they agree to pay you fifty thousand dollars if your house burns down. They're hoping that it'll never burn, or that if it does, it'll be after you've paid in more than fifty thousand dollars."

"That's dumb," I said. "Wouldn't it be better to put five hundred dollars in the bank every three months, to have in case your house burned down?"

"It would if you could plan when it was going to burn," said Mom, "but you don't want it to burn at all, and if it does, it could be next week. If that happens, you've only paid five hundred, but the insurance still has to pay fifty thousand."

"But that makes it a good thing if your house burns down," I protested. Sometimes I think grown-ups don't have any sense, the way they set things up.

"No, because fifty thousand dollars is about what your house was worth," said Mom. "You come out about even."

"Of course, something like that adobe house, you could come out ahead," said Dad. "As far as I know, the Wellers didn't have any plans to fix it up, and they couldn't tear it down because it got on to that historical list. It was sitting there using up taxes and insurance, and whatever value the insurance companies and the tax assessors put on it was completely theoretical. Now the house is probably burned badly enough to be condemned, and they can tear it down and put in a parking lot till property values go up. That won't cost much, it'll bring their taxes way down, and they'll probably have some money left over to sock into their other properties."

"Well, I hope they sock it into the Brick House," said Mom. "I want to fix that place up so badly I can taste it."

CHAPTER ELEVEN

Donnavita Detects

ROXANNE PRACTICALLY HAD STEAM COMING OUT her ears at the bus stop next morning. She walked up to Heather and said, "You tell that brother of yours it's not nice to talk about people behind their backs."

"He didn't," said Heather. "He thought you had permission to be out of school so it was okay to talk about it."

"You're the one telling lies, Roxy," said Donnavita, miserably. "Where do you get off being mad at Marshall?"

"Where do you get off believing him instead of me?" For a minute I was afraid Roxanne would hit her with her book bag.

"You've told lies before," Donnavita pointed out.

"Marshall never has, and he doesn't have a reason to, anyway. But you do."

Roxanne looked sideways at Heather. "I didn't say he was lying. He could be confused. Anyway, it's none of your business what I do."

We Burglars were quiet for a while after we got onto the bus. Rainbow spoke up first. "So what happened?"

"I asked her why she was ditching school," said Donnavita. "I've heard people would automatically tell the truth, if you asked why or how they did something, instead of whether they did it. Only it didn't work. She says she isn't ditching."

We looked at Heather. "Marshall might get confused about days or time," she said, "but not about people. If she bothered to tell him she had permission to be out of school, he must've seen her on a school day."

"She might have all kinds of reasons to skip school that don't have anything to do with fires," said Rainbow.

"Right," said Donnavita, "but there's only one way to find out if she won't tell me. I'll have to tail her."

"But—that'd mean cutting school yourself," I said.

Donnavita rolled her eyes at me as if I were being dumb. "You got any better ideas?"

"We'll make you a disguise," said Rainbow.

"I'll write you a note," said Heather, who has the most grown-up handwriting.

"How are you going to tail her?" I asked. "She could be long gone by now."

"I don't think so," said Donnavita. "If she ditched all day, somebody'd call Mom and Dad. If Heather gets me out of the last two periods, I can hang around the high school until she shows up."

I felt a little sick to my stomach about it, but I didn't have any good ideas, so I helped. We could have disguised her better if we'd had the model case, or if it had been cooler and we'd had sweaters and hats to change. I changed blouses with her in the rest room between classes, and we braided her hair, and Rainbow got some stiff cardboard from her art class and cut out a visor for her. We wanted to get her some high-heeled shoes to change her height, but all the girls in our class wear tennis shoes. She still looked like Donnavita when we were done, but at least she didn't look like the same Donnavita that Roxanne saw that morning. Heather wrote a note to get her out of classes to go to the dentist, and she walked out at the beginning of science.

(Mom read this and asked, "Does Heather write these notes often?" Of course not! We only ever ditch school in an emergency. Grown-ups have such suspicious minds. Mom read this too, and said she'd never been suspicious, but never would not be suspicious now. Which I guess is fair.)

All the rest of us could do was worry about Donnavita, and that would be boring to read, so what we did so I could write this chapter is, Donnavita told what happened into a tape recorder, and Mom and I are copying it out. This is called transcribing. So after this for a while everything will be like Donnavita tells it, except we cut out a lot of "uhs" and giggles.

This is Donnavita. I'm glad I'm going to be a model when I grow up and not a detective, because tailing people is mega-boring. When I got to the high school I was nervous and kind of scared. I walked all around the high school and you would not believe how many doors it has. There was no telling which would be best to sneak out by, and I couldn't watch them all. I was already nervous that I'd missed her.

So I tried to think like a detective. I knew from Marshall that at least sometimes she goes home, so I walked back to the bus stop, which is a couple of blocks away, and you can't see the high school from it. First I waited right at the stop, but I had to keep shaking my head at the drivers to let them know they didn't have to stop for me, and when Roxanne came she'd be able to see me before I saw her, and I didn't want that. So I moved.

I climbed onto the concrete wall of a flower bed for the bank that's right there, and that's when it got boring. I didn't have anything to do except my homework. It felt like everybody who went by stared at me, wondering why I wasn't in school. Every two seconds I'd look out from under my visor, trying to see Roxanne. It felt like I sat there forever.

When Roxanne finally came by I almost missed her! She'd already passed the bus stop and was walking down the sidewalk right past me when I looked up. I fell back into the flower bed, dropping my homework. If she'd looked up, she'd've seen me for sure; but she didn't. I had to pick up my homework then, so she was a whole block ahead of me by the time I started to follow her. Which I guess was a good thing. I hurried to catch up, then remembered I shouldn't catch up, and slowed down too much, so I almost lost her at a traffic light. She was walking pretty fast, but lucky for me she was going in a straight line, except she turned at Houston Street. I think it was Houston Street. I was pretty lost till finally I saw the Santa Rosa Hospital, where I had my tonsils out. Then I knew right where we were. We'd walked halfway home already.

While I was waiting for a traffic light, Roxanne went into the park and sat down on a bench next to another girl. On the map this park is called Milam Square, but we call it the *Campo Santo*. This is Spanish for holy ground. It used to be a graveyard, so now it's full of guardian angels for the kids in the hospital. They took away the headstones when they made the park, and put up walls instead, with the names of the buried people on metal plates on the walls. I figured if I hid behind one of the walls, near the bench Roxanne was on, I'd be able to hear what she and the other girl were saying.

It would've worked, too, if they'd just sat still. But by the time I got close enough to see that the other girl was Dahomey Jackson, she was getting up and walking toward the other end of the park. I had to follow them all the way to the statue of Ben Milam (who is a hero from the Texas Revolution, but I don't have time to go into that now), ducking from wall to wall and only catching a bit here and there.

"Don't you see I can't?" shouted Dahomey.

And Roxanne yelled back, "Don't you see you can't go on like this anymore?"

And a little later, she said, "Even if Marshall hadn't seen me, Mom and Dad would start noticing how fast we're using up groceries pretty soon. You're lucky he didn't see *you*!"

So now I'd started to figure it out. Did Mary Jane say before about Dahomey Jackson disappearing? If she didn't she should have. Roxanne must've known where she was all the time and been ditching school to bring her stuff to eat. She would be in mega-trouble for this if I told, but it was lots better than her being a pyro. They wound up arguing right under the Milam statue, too far from the walls to do me any good, so I decided to circle around the statue and hide behind the pedestal. Roxanne saw me while I was doing the circling around, and my disguise was no good at all. The first thing she did was screech, "Donnavita! What're you doing here?"

I jumped, but Roxanne doesn't scare me. Much. "Finding out what you're doing here," I said. "I knew you were lying."

"Great!" said Dahomey. "Just great! I don't have a choice now, do I?"

"Maybe," said Roxanne. "Donnavita, if you tell any-body—"

"I have to tell the Burg—Heather and Rainbow and Mary Jane," I said. "They helped me get out of school and make my disguise."

"Oh, is that what that is?" Roxanne's good at sounding disgusted.

Dahomey looked like maybe she was going to cry. "Oh, fine. That tears it. Either I go home or I run all the way to Mexico."

"We can keep secrets," I said.

"Three can keep a secret if two of them are dead," said Dahomey. "Six can't keep a secret at all."

"And there's no point in going to Mexico," Roxanne told her. "Your Spanish stinks. It's time to give yourself up."

"What'd you do?" I asked. "And where've you been staying?"

"None of your business," said Roxanne.

Dahomey told me anyway while we waited for the bus. She was the one who got the dope that started the fire in the rest room. Her dad is a cop, and she was sure he'd kill her. Plus, he's real good at asking questions, because his job is getting people to tell him things they don't want to say. He'd want to know who sold her the grass. She'd got it from Los Red Dukes (I think the only reason they show up at school is so they can push dope), and she was afraid to finger them, because the first person she had run into leaving that rest room was Jimmy Losoya. He'd grabbed her arm and put his face up next to hers and said in this low, scary voice, "You tell your dad, you're dead meat." He could do it too. Los Red Dukes carry switchblades, and one of them was expelled for pulling one on a teacher.

So she ran. She'd been wandering all over town for however many days now, sleeping in parks and trying not to spend her money. She didn't have any clothes or anything, and she was afraid she'd wind up having to take a bus to Mexico. Roxanne had been cutting her last period, which is only study hall and easy to sneak out of, to bring Dahomey food. She'd even brought her home to get a shower once, the day Marshall saw her.

"But it's all over now, thanks to you, squirt," said Dahomey. "So if Jimmy cuts me up, you remember it's your fault!"

"And if you think I won't tell Mom and Dad about you following me, you've got another think coming," said Roxanne.

"That's okay," I said. "I won't be in any worse trouble than you."

I got off at the stop across from the Brick House, and they went on, because they were going straight to Dahomey's folks. If I had sat at the bus stop and waited for the rest of the Burglars, this story would've gone different, but I decided to go in. As I walked past the Brick House I saw Mr. TJ's BMW parked in the side street, and the gate and the door were open.

I looked in the front door. Last time Mr. TJ hadn't found any of our secret stuff, but all he had to do was go to the Treasure Room and look in the window seat, and Rainbow'd left the cat bowls sitting out in Isis's room. Maybe I should go in and distract him? While I was thinking about it, he came out, carrying a big briefcase. He looked surprised to see me, and slammed the door shut.

"Hi, Mr. TJ," I said.

I could tell the minute he recognized me. "Why, hi, Donnavita," he said, coming closer. "I almost didn't know you. You should leave your hair loose; it's so pretty that way."

"I usually do," I said. People remember my face, but hardly anybody gets my name right, so I decided to like him and ask what we most wanted to know. "Will you fix up the Brick House?"

Mr. TJ shook his head. "Probably not. These old houses are so expensive to keep up; and I don't think my dad likes the idea. Sorry. It would've been nice to fill it with video games and things, wouldn't it?" All the time he talked he was padlocking the gate, unlocking his car, and dumping the briefcase in the backseat. "I'm running late. Say hi to your folks for me."

After he drove off I went to my apartment. Jimmy was in the parking lot with a couple of Los Red Dukes, doing something to a motorbike. I ignored them and went in for a snack.

And now Mary Jane can have the story back.

CHAPTER TWELVE
The Second Fire

THE PARKING LOT WAS EMPTY AND DONNAVITA
was at the bus stop eating an apple when we got home.
We pounced on her, but all she said was, "It's okay
about Roxanne, but not about the house. I'll tell you
at the meeting."

So we hurried to put our stuff up and meet at the
fence. Marshall came with Heather. "He says Isis is
acting funny," she told us, not frowning exactly, but
pulling her eyebrows down. "She wouldn't eat her cat
food, and kept running back and forth crying at him."

"She cried a lot," Marshall said, to be sure we under-
stood.

"Maybe Mr. TJ upset her," said Donnavita. "He was
coming out when I came home."

We all looked at the Brick House. The house stood

quiet and abandoned as ever, except that, as we watched, Isis climbed out the window with Sunshine in her mouth. Sunshine was almost too big to carry, and she was having a heck of a time with him.

"Something's wrong," said Heather, and climbed the fence. We followed her, except Marshall, who said, "I'll stand watch!"

As soon as we saw Isis's room we had two signs something was wrong. One, the mattress was gone. Two, the house smelled smoky. We yelped and scattered. I don't remember who went where or said what, but I remember Rainbow pounding up the stairs yelling, "The closet under the stairs!"

The mattress was on fire, half in and half out of the closet. Heather brought the fire extinguisher. We stomped on sparks with our feet, and Donnavita and I knocked over the roll of carpet and rolled it back and forth on the mattress. Rainbow tore open the carton of milk she'd brought for the kittens and splashed it on the wall where the wallpaper had caught, then took off her T-shirt and swatted at the little wormy flames that kept eating at the edges of the burned place. We all coughed and choked and our eyes watered, and you wouldn't believe how hard that carpet was to roll, but finally the fire was out.

The hall was a mess. Fire extinguishers spit out this white foamy stuff that gets all over everything. (Not that I'm complaining.) The hole in the mattress was much bigger, the stuffing that wasn't burned spilling out onto the floor. You could see blackened boards in the wall where the wallpaper'd burned off. The floor and the closet looked like somebody turned over a trash can, except that most of the trash was newspapers and spray-paint cans. "Los Red Dukes" was spray painted on the walls four or five times.

We were shaking all over. " Jimmy," said Donnavita, coughing and waving the old smoke away from her face. "It's got to be Jimmy. I saw Mr. TJ leave when I got home from tailing Roxanne, and Jimmy and some of Los Dukes were in the parking lot."

"But how'd he get in?" I asked.

Donnavita glared at the front door. "I saw Mr. TJ come out. He banged the door, but I don't remember him locking it."

Heather marched over and tried the knob. It turned, and she opened the door easily. Marshall, pacing up and down, saw her at once. He hurried to the gate; she made the "okay" sign by making her thumb and index finger into a circle and holding them up, and shut the door again.

"Quick emergency meeting, y'all," she said. "And then we need to clean ourselves up before our folks get home."

Isis was still trying to get Bib outside when we went back up. Rainbow caught her and tried to calm her down, but was too scared still to do it right. We were all a mess, but Rainbow was the worst, with her T-shirt ruined. (Donnavita and I traded blouses again about this time.) Heather opened the meeting, and Donnavita gave us the short version of what had gone on with her, including the bad news about Mr. TJ not thinking the rec center would come through.

"We've got to go straight to Mr. Sanchez," I said. "This time we know it's Jimmy."

Heather shook her head. "It won't work."

"Why not?" howled Rainbow. "He practically signed his name!"

"That's not proof," said Heather. "Remember what Roxanne told Donnavita? You have to catch them in the act. If Donnavita'd been watching the house—"

"You can't blame me for that," grumbled Donnavita. "I didn't know he was going to try again today."

"We can't keep watch on the house all the time," I said.

"I can," said Rainbow.

We looked at her.

"I can, really," she said. "Domie's always complaining about how schools kill a kid's personality. So I'll just stay out of school and watch till I catch Jimmy setting a fire."

"You can't get into the house by yourself," I said.

"I can if the door's not locked."

"It'll be mega-boring," warned Donnavita.

"Unless he sees you," I said. "Then it'll be way too exciting. He could cut you up, or—"

"I don't care! Somebody's got to catch him before he burns up the house and all the cats!"

We argued, and we should've taken a vote, but we had to cut the meeting short to get cleaned up before people's folks got off work (or in Heather's case, got

101

out of bed). I had foam in my hair, and we all smelled like smoke. When we crossed the parking lot (I went to Donnavita's to wash), I kept hoping Mom would look out. If she saw us like this, we'd have to tell her what was going on.

She did wonder how come I came home with my hair wet. I told her we'd been playing with water balloons, which I think is the only flat-out lie I'd told yet. I was kind of cranky and impatient with Sloop, partly because I felt lousy, but partly hoping Mom would notice and bug me about what was the matter with me, so I'd have an excuse to let something slip. Mom had other things to think about, though.

"I called Mr. Weller today," she said, as she passed the biscuits at suppertime.

"And what'd he say?" asked Dad.

"Mr. TJ never talked to him about turning the Brick House into a rec center." Mom sounded disgusted. I stopped making faces at Sloop, and started paying attention. "Never mentioned it—can you believe it?"

"Maybe Mr. Weller was just shifting the blame for not doing anything," suggested Dad.

Mom shook her head, cutting up Sloop's meat with fierce motions. "He thinks it's a great idea. He's sending a couple of people around first thing Monday."

"That's funny," I said. "Mr. TJ told Donnavita he didn't think he'd get to fix up the Brick House, because Mr. Weller didn't think it'd work."

Mom looked at me with her eyebrows raised. "He did? When?"

102

"Today. She . . . uh . . . got off early and met him coming out of the Brick House. Didn't he come say hi to you?"

"No. Dang him!" Mom banged down her knife and passed Sloop his plate almost as if it were a football. "He's done nothing but give me the runaround since the meeting. Tomorrow I'm calling Mr. TJ up and giving him a piece of my mind!"

"You'll be all over your mad in the morning," said Dad. "Call him tonight."

"I think I will," said Mom.

We barely had the table cleared, though, when the phone rang. Dad got it; and I could tell in the first couple of sentences that he was talking to Mr. Barracotta. "Um . . . there's something I should tell you," I said to Mom, as we scraped plates.

"Oh? What's that?"

"I helped Donnavita cut school so she could spy on Roxanne today."

Mom stared at me. "You what?"

"It was in a good cause," I said. "Am I grounded?"

It wound up we all were, except Rainbow. We were so grounded, we couldn't even call each other on the phone, which is why we didn't know what went on with Rainbow till the next morning; but that's all going to be in the next chapter.

The only other thing that happened that night was Mom called Mr. TJ at his house and chewed him out. I felt kind of sorry for him. She didn't call him a liar, because he's sort of her boss; but she was plenty mad.

"Can you believe he hinted around that Mr. Weller's getting senile?" she said after she hung up. "Tried to tell me his dad was confused when I talked to him. Confused! His old man's body may be going, but his mind's as steady as ever."

"I'm glad it's Mr. Weller who signs the checks," said Dad, "but you should remember, it could be TJ doing it, any day now."

"I don't think Mr. Weller's in danger anymore," said Mom, "but I've got a good mind to start hunting for another job if he goes into the hospital again." She sat down on the couch and put her feet in Dad's lap. "Ooof! This has been some week! Fires and runaways and people yelling at each other—and my quiet, good daughter lending her aid and her blouse in cutting school!"

"Mary Jane's in trouble, Mary Jane's in trouble," chanted Sloop.

"And Sloop'll be in trouble, too, if he doesn't pick up his toys," said Mom.

Sloop started pushing his dump truck around the living room, loading his blocks and G.I. Joe and stuff into it. I was feeling all heavy and sick inside. "I had to do it," I said, sitting on the edge of the couch. "Donnavita was real worried about Roxanne, and this was the only way she could think of to find out what was going on."

"You've got to admit it turned out all right," said Dad, hooking his arm around me and dragging me into his lap. "If the Jackson kid's going to finger

Jimmy for her dad, maybe something'll be done about that situation, finally."

Mom sounded real tired. "It won't be enough," she said, "and it doesn't change the fact that helping Donnavita to cut school was wrong. But we do understand why you did it, baby." Mom dragged her mouth up into a smile. "When I think of all the things other parents have to punish their kids for, it doesn't seem like you and Sloop are ever bad, to speak of."

I felt like slime.

CHAPTER THIRTEEN

Rainbow Detects

TRANSCRIBING IS A BIGGER PAIN THAN YOU'D think, but we're doing it again, because Rainbow was by herself when this happened, and if I tell you about it, it's hearsay. So this is what happened to Rainbow that Thursday night:

Hi. This is Rainbow. After we put out the fire I took a shower and changed and took my T-shirt to the Dumpster so Domie and Petal wouldn't see it. They're not as uptight as most grown-ups, but they'd notice a burned shirt. The other girls tell me they were scared and shaky and Mary Jane felt guilty (of course) but all I was was mad. It was bad enough Jimmy sold dope and wrote his gang's name all over everything and made so much noise at night a person couldn't sleep.

Burning down houses with things living in them, even if it's cats instead of people, was just too much. I wasn't going to let him get away with it.

Domie and Petal are always tired when they get home, and fight over whose turn it is to cook. I could cook just fine if they'd let me. They asked me what I'd done that day, and I sat on the bar stool while Petal cooked fish sticks and Domie set the bar. (We don't have a table.) And I told them about Donnavita.

"You're going to help her catch up on the classes she missed, right?" asked Petal.

"Oh, sure," I said.

"Then that's all right," said Petal. "I hope Roxanne realizes how lucky she is, to have a sister that cares enough to go to all that trouble. My sisters would've told on me and let the chips fall."

I've never seen any of my great-aunts. Petal only had one kid on purpose, because she'd hated having sisters so much.

"Hey, you remember that time I skipped school to go to the antiwar demonstration?" said Domie. "I wasn't any older'n you, Rainbow, and they didn't want to let me into the picket line. Kept telling me to get back to school. So I stole a sign and wrote 'War Protesters Unfair to Kids' on the back of it, and walked up and down the other side of the street. Why weren't you at that protest, Petal?"

"I was working," said Petal. "Even activists have to eat."

They can go on and on like this forever. I wish people

in San Antonio protested things now. We hung up a sign that said "No Blood for Oil" during the Gulf War, but that's not as good as a real protest, with people marching and stuff.

Anyway, when Mr. Barracotta called to tell Domie about my helping Donnavita, she told him she knew all about it and thought I'd done right and he should be glad Donnavita had that much gumption ba-blah ba-blah ba-blah. Other kids think Domie's cool, but other grown-ups can't stand her.

So we did dishes and played Chinese checkers and I did my homework and we went to bed; and in the middle of the night I woke up. I'd gone to sleep thinking about how I was going to keep an eye on Jimmy, so I guess I was psyched; I could tell right away it was his motorbike coming home that woke me, even if I didn't hear it anymore.

Domie and I sleep in the living room on the Hide-A-Bed. All I had to do to look out was go to the armchair under the front window. Most likely Jimmy'd go inside to bed—but I looked out anyway. I figured I might as well get in the habit. Three or four Red Dukes were hanging around the door to his apartment, passing a joint one way down the line and a bottle the other way, talking in Spanglish, laughing and making motions like they were telling stories—not very nice stories, I didn't think. It was a warm night, so I wasn't uncomfortable, but I was pretty sleepy and it was hard to pay attention.

Finally one Duke threw the bottle down so it broke

on the pavement, and they got on their motorbikes and drove off as loud as they could. I thought: Good. Now Jimmy'll go inside and I can go back to bed, but he reached into his jacket and brought out a baggie and some paper, and started to roll a new joint.

I was so tired I had to put my head down on the back of the armchair. I guess I fell asleep, because I woke up with a jerk. Jimmy was walking past the window, with the end of the joint glowing like a bike reflector between his fingers. He slouched along down the row of buildings till he got about halfway, and then he started cutting across toward the Brick House.

Suddenly I was wide awake. I slid out of the armchair so fast I thumped when I hit the floor. It sounded loud to me, but Domie didn't wake up. I was more careful taking the chain off the door and letting myself out. I almost pulled the door all the way shut (if you do that it locks itself), but stopped in time.

Jimmy was almost to the Brick House. Figuring bare feet wouldn't make any noise, I ran across the parking lot. There was enough light I didn't worry about the broken glass and stuff, and blacktop doesn't hurt much, if it's cool. I felt like I was wide awake, but probably if I had been I'd've planned it better, got myself some cover. By the time I started thinking about how to watch him without being seen, he'd reached the fence at the back of the Brick House and stood looking at it, sucking on the joint. I wondered if he were wondering why his fire hadn't taken, and I wondered if he'd see me if I ran real fast to the first live

109

oak. But before I could try, he took one last pull on the joint, dropped the end, and stepped on it, and turned. We both jumped, and I guess he got some of the smoke down the wrong way because he choked and coughed. I froze—didn't even think of running away! When Jimmy got done choking he said, real mad, "What you want to sneak up on me for?"

"Sorry," I said, automatically. "I didn't do it on purpose." Which was true; I didn't want him to catch me.

"So what did you do on purpose?" he asked. "Your mama'll hide you, out running around in your nightie."

"It covers everything," I said, getting my mad back. My "nightie" is a long T-shirt of Petal's, with a cat face on it, and comes down to my knees.

"What are you doing out here?" He came a step closer to me, and I remembered he'd been drinking and smoking dope and probably wasn't thinking as clearly as he thought he was. There was no telling what he might do.

I took a step back and heard my voice go funny. "What are *you* doing out here?" I asked, instead of answering.

His hand moved fast as a snake and grabbed my arm. "You're spying on me, aren't you?" He put his face down even with mine. "You sneaky little kid. What you got against me?"

"Nothing!" I gulped. His breath stunk.

"You talked to those fire marshals about me."

"Did not! I didn't tell them anything about anybody!"

"Everybody's saying I torched that house. Los Red Dukes don't do no torching, I told them that, but you been telling them I did, you and your snotty little friends."

"We did not!" I said. "And even if we did, so what? They're going to catch you one way or the other."

"Los Red Dukes don't do no torching!" He shook me, and his voice sounded funny, I mean even funnier than it did anyway from the dope.

I tried to pull away. "Let go of me!"

"Ain't nobody believes me," he said, hanging on tighter. "I ever catch one of my Dukes torching, I'll cut him up so bad his own mama won't know him. Why don't nobody believe me?"

"Why should we?" I was losing my temper and maybe my good sense. "You cut people up and push dope and steal things and write your gang name all over everything. Why shouldn't you burn houses down too?"

"Listen." He pushed his face up close. "I knew a kid, he had two little sisters, and he was supposed to watch them, and he didn't, and they played with matches and caught their clothes and the bed on fire. And their hair—their hair was all burning." He talked real fast, and he didn't blink. That was kind of gross. His eyes were right opposite mine, not blinking. I didn't look away. I was waiting for them to blink, and they never did. "He burned his arms all up, trying to put his little sisters out. They had him in the hospital for months. They had to take skin off of his side and stick it on his arms, 'cause the skin on his arms was all burned away. But his little sisters, there wasn't enough skin in the world to help them."

I looked down at the sleeves of his leather jacket he never takes off, not even last summer when it got to 108 degrees. He shoved me away. "Los Red Dukes don't do no torching," he said. "You go tell everybody that. Now you get back to bed."

I ran home, and I didn't look back.

CHAPTER FOURTEEN
Stakeout

RAINBOW TOLD US ABOUT JIMMY AT THE BUS
stop, so Roxanne heard it, too. "Oh, that's so sad," she
said. "No wonder he's such a creep."

"Even if that story really was about him and not
somebody else like he said, it's no excuse for pushing
dope," said Donnavita. "Don't you and Dahomey go
feeling sorry for him and back out of testifying."

"Too late," said Roxanne. "She already told her dad."

So that was good, but we couldn't talk about the real
problem till we Burglars got onto the bus. "So you
believe that about his sisters and Los Red Dukes never
setting fires?" Heather asked Rainbow.

Rainbow nodded. "You'd believe, too, if you'd been
there."

"But that leaves us right back where we started!" complained Donnavita. "There's nobody left."

"Oh," I said. Suddenly my brain was going *click, click, click*, like when you finally understand how a math problem's supposed to work.

The others looked at me. "Oh, what?" asked Heather.

"It's Mr. TJ," I said. "There's nobody else it could be."

"That's dumb," said Rainbow. "It's his house."

At least, that's what she says she said. All I could hear was the *click, click, click* in my head. I jumped up and rang the bell for the next stop. "And he's going to try again today!"

"What?" said Donnavita.

I had to talk fast. "He never talked to Mr. Weller about fixing the Brick House up, but Mom did! And Mr. Weller likes the idea, and he's sending people to look at it Monday."

"Mary Jane, what are you doing?" Heather demanded as the bus slowed.

"We've got to catch him!"

"Are you out of your mind?" squeaked Donnavita. "We're already grounded!"

"So?" The door opened. "Come on!"

"Come on where? And do what?"

"I'll tell you on the way."

Rainbow stood up.

"Sit down," said Heather. "There's better ways to do this."

114

"You don't even know what I'm doing," I objected.

"And I'm not helping till I do," said Heather.

"You getting off or not?" asked the driver.

I hopped out of the bus and waved for them to come after me, but Heather shook her head, and the door closed.

I crossed the street and caught the next bus toward home, afraid Mr. TJ would get there before me. I didn't see the BMW in front of the house when I got off the bus, though. What I did see was Sloop, riding his trike in front of our apartment. If I came up the driveway and climbed the fence to our secret entrance, he'd see me for sure.

I hid behind a live oak and waited. The trouble with little kids is they can do the same thing over and over again forever without getting bored. He'd ride to one end of the building, making *vroom-vroom* noises, turn around, and ride to the other end. Half the time he had his back to me, but I wasn't sure that half of the time would be long enough for me to get into the Brick House. I wondered if you could die from frustration.

Finally I decided to make a run for it. The next time Sloop turned his back I was ready. The fence rattled something awful, but I didn't have time to worry about it. I scrambled to the roof and in at the window, hearing Sloop yell as I ducked inside.

The kittens ran up to me. Poor things. They were having to sleep on the floor now the mattress was all burned. Isis was off somewhere. I heard Mom and Sloop talking, but couldn't understand what they said. If Mom caught me, would she believe me and mount guard on the house herself? I couldn't count on it. Everything was up to me now.

The air smelled slightly smoky, but it must have been left over from the burned mattress, because I searched the whole house and didn't find any fire. The kittens followed me.

In the Treasure Room, I stretched out on the window seat, where I could raise my head slightly and see onto the street without being seen myself, I hoped. I told myself I was a detective on a stakeout; but nothing happened, and I started to feel like a kid cutting school.

My stomach began to ache. What was I doing here all alone? It wouldn't've hurt to stay on the bus another couple of stops and explain what I'd figured out to the others. Detectives on stakeouts, I remembered, always have partners.

I remembered a movie I'd seen part of once, where a kid had seen a crime committed, and the bad guy was chasing him down to kill him before he could tell. I really couldn't picture Mr. TJ doing that—but a week ago I couldn't've pictured him burning down the Brick House, either.

Sunshine and Boots were wrestling in the fireplace. Bib was trying to climb up to me, and Nyota had curled up in a chunk of sunlight on the floor. I slid off the window seat, opened it up, got out my minutes book, and got back on the lid, bringing Bib with me. I was going to leave some evidence, just in case.

First I wrote down all about Rainbow and Jimmy and Mom and Mr. Weller, and then I wrote this:

What I figure is going on is Mr. TJ has been meaning to burn down the Brick House and get the insurance. Probably he burned the other house, too, and sprayed Los Red Dukes's name all over to make people suspect them. Anyway, that house he could burn down in the middle of the night, because nobody lived near it. But he's trying to burn this one down in the daytime. Maybe he wants to be sure Mr. Sanchez could put out the fire before it gets to the apartments and kills anybody. It's also pretty dead around here in the daytime, and even if anybody saw him (which Marshall and Donnavita both did), he could say he was inspecting the Brick House. At night he couldn't say that. I bet he even left the door open on purpose, so the police could figure a way for somebody else to get in and set the fire. If he comes on the weekend, people are running in and out all day, instead of being at school or at work. And Mr. Weller's going to send in workers and inspectors on Monday. So if Mr. TJ wants to burn the Brick House, he has to do it today, Friday, and that's why I'm here.

It took a while to write all this. I was making the letters big and readable, in case the book got scorched, and I kept looking out the window in case Mr. TJ drove up; and Bib thought the moving pen was a game, which is why there are claw marks all over the minutes book. Once when I looked out I saw Mr. Sanchez standing in front of the Brick House and frowning at it. I ducked as soon as I saw him, and next time I looked he was gone.

Nothing happened then for a long time. I played with the kittens until Isis came looking for them and they all went to her for lunch. They had food in their bowls from yesterday, but they were still drinking milk from her, too. So then I looked at the scrapbooks in the window seat and read ahead in my English book and tried to work on a story in the front of the minutes book, but it's hard to write a story when you're looking out the window every two minutes. I couldn't hear a thing from the street with the windows closed, and I was afraid if I opened one Mr. TJ would see and be warned.

I ate the cookies from my lunch and looked at Donnavita's magazines, and felt sicker and sicker, afraid Mr. TJ wouldn't show up. I'd be in such incredible trouble, and I'd either have to lie, or get everybody else in trouble, too, telling the truth. (I never for one minute thought I would be able to cut a whole day of school and not get caught.) I reminded myself that the other times Mr. TJ hadn't shown up till late afternoon, but that didn't make me feel any better. It meant I could be here an awful long time, and being in the Brick House by myself wasn't near as much fun as being there with the other Burglars.

After I'd eaten my lunch and the cats had fallen asleep in a heap, I realized I hadn't looked out the window in a while. So I looked, and the BMW was parked in the street like it belonged there. I couldn't see Mr. TJ, but as I wondered if he'd gotten in without my noticing, I heard the door opening downstairs.

Isis had looked asleep, but she jumped up with her eyes as wide and round as if they never had been shut.

"He's here," I told her, "but don't worry. I won't let him burn your babies." I picked up the minutes book and tiptoed down the hall, terrified he'd hear me, but he was making plenty of noise of his own. I heard him swear, and bang stuff around. I went to Isis's window and threw my minutes book out as hard as I could. It landed on the porch roof, which was not the idea, but I didn't really think Mr. TJ would kill me, anyway. I'd just pretended to myself that I did to make it more interesting.

Isis crouched at the head of the stairs, lashing her tail. Walking as softly as I could, I tiptoed down, hunched behind the banisters, until I could see Mr. TJ.

Mr. TJ had on an apron over his suit, and white trash bags over his hands, fastened at the elbows with rubber bands. As I watched, he took a stack of newspaper out of the briefcase, which stood open at the foot of the stairs, and started throwing it around. Then he took a big square bottle out of the case and unscrewed the lid, having trouble because of the trash bags on his hands. When he started splashing it around, I recognized the stink. It was turpentine, like the workers use when they repaint an apartment. Mom always warns Sloop and me away from it, because it's poisonous and flammable.

I noticed that I hadn't planned what to do at this point. Donnavita said that Roxanne said you practically had to see somebody light a fire to arrest them for it, but if I waited till Mr. TJ lit the match, he might get away before I could bring anyone. With all that turpentine around, the whole hall could be on fire before I got out of the building. I decided I'd better go get somebody. There couldn't be any doubt of what was going on now. Mom and Mr. Sanchez would have to believe me.

I started to back up the stairs, and I stepped on Isis. Isis screamed.

I ran, my feet sounding like thunder on the stairs. Mr. TJ ran after me shouting, "Who's there?"

I was almost to Isis's window when he caught me, one trash-bagged hand grabbing my arm. I fought, but he grabbed my other arm and held me tight, even when I tried to kick him. You can't kick very well in tennis shoes.

"What are you doing out of school, young lady?" he demanded.

CHAPTER FIFTEEN
Accusations

WHEN I REMEMBER IT NOW, IT'S FUNNY. THERE he was, caught red-handed, getting turpentine all over my T-shirt, and he acted like he just saw me on the street when I was supposed to be in school! For a minute I goggled at him.

"Well?" he said, like any normal grown-up. "I'm waiting."

"I came to catch you burning down the Brick House," I said. "And I did! I'll tell Mr. Sanchez, and he'll tell your dad and the fire marshal, and you'll go to jail and even"—I didn't like the way he was looking at me one bit—"even if you kill me, Heather and Rainbow and Donnavita know all about it, too!"

I figured that'd fix him, but he looked disgusted. "I

told Dad we should have a no-kids policy," he said. "Downstairs, Mary Jane. March!"

I was so surprised I did as he said. He twisted my arm up behind my back, which hurt. "This will break your mother's heart, you know," he said, as if he'd caught me stealing.

"You're talking like I'm the one who did something wrong," I said. "I mean, I know it's bad to cut school, but it's nothing compared to what you're doing."

"I'm checking out an old house to see what's necessary for its renovation," he said. We stepped around the briefcase.

"Yeah, right," I said, trying to sound hard and sarcastic like somebody from a movie. I felt all queasy and jittery, and I expect it showed. "Everybody splashes turpentine all over houses when they inspect them."

"None of your lip," said Mr. TJ, dragging me into the hall.

We weren't but five feet from the front door. I figured this was my chance. "Let go of me!" I shouted, twisting, and stomping on his foot as hard as I could. I almost got free, but he hooked his foot around my ankle, letting go of my arms, so I fell *thump!* on the floor. While I rolled over and scrambled around in the wet newspapers, getting to my feet, he tore off his trash bags and started undoing the apron with one hand, getting a box of matches out of the pocket with the other. He'd put himself between me and the door now. He couldn't grab with both hands full, but he could trip me. I ran toward the kitchen.

I expected him to run after me, but he was too busy lighting matches. I flew straight through the kitchen. The door to the screen porch was locked with a dead bolt. I opened that, and ran onto the porch. That door had one of those knobs with the bump that you turn to lock and unlock it. As I turned it I saw Mr. Sanchez open his door and look out.

"Mr. Sanchez!" I screamed, hearing running behind me.

He heard me. I could see him looking around. "F-i-i-i-i-i-i-r-e!" I cried, dragging the word out as long as I could.

That got Mr. Sanchez's attention. He ran toward the Brick House. I got through the porch door and ran to the fence, shouting, "The front hall!" (I see now this wasn't very helpful, but it was all I thought of at the time, if you can call what I was doing thinking.) I saw Mom open our apartment door. Mr. TJ ran after me, catching onto me as I threw one leg over the top of the fence. "Sanchez!" he shouted. "Quick! This kid's set the house on fire!"

"Liar! You did it!" I shouted, kicking at his face and falling over the other side of the fence. I landed hard.

Did you ever get the wind knocked out of you? It hurts! I couldn't hear or see or think anything, it hurt so bad!

I don't think I stayed like that long, but when I could make sense of the world again Mom and Sloop were kneeling by me, and I could hear a whole bunch of people shouting. The first thing I thought of was Mr.

123

TJ blaming me for his fire. "I didn't do it," I told Mom, gasping, because I still hadn't got all my air back. "It was Mr. TJ. I can prove it." Then I thought of a bunch of things at once. "Isis! You've got to get the kittens out! And the minutes book's on top of the porch—"

"It's okay," said Mom. "They're putting the fire out."

"*They* who?" I asked. "Don't let Mr. TJ do it. He'll destroy evidence."

Sloop was looking at me all this time with wide, scared eyes, like he gets if you tell him about the Donkey Lady. "Are you a ghost?" he asked. "You looked dead."

"I'm fine," I said. "You don't know how dead people look."

He hugged me, which was the last thing in the world I expected. "I'm glad," he said. "If you were dead you couldn't tell Mom you went through that window. I saw you, but she wouldn't believe me. Tell her how you went in the window."

"All right, Sloop, I believe you now," said Mom. She sounded kind of mad, but I couldn't tell at who. She helped me to my feet. "Let's go inside. I have to call Mr. Weller."

I walked backward all the way in and stayed at the window while she called, trying to figure out what was going on at the Brick House. Everything seemed to be happening around front, out of sight. The people at the bus stop were all standing up, looking at something and waving their arms and talking, so you could tell something interesting was going on. I didn't see any smoke, but I smelled it.

After she called Mr. Weller, Mom called the fire marshal. "It's clearly a case of arson," she said. "We even have two suspects for you. . . . My daughter, and one of the landlords. . . . Of course I don't believe it's my daughter! She's got a lot of explaining to do, though, and I don't expect you to take my word for it. . . . Don't worry, we'll be waiting for you."

After she hung up she walked over to me and said, "Okay, young lady. Go change your clothes, and we'll talk."

I was all covered with turpentine from Mr. TJ knocking me into the newspapers. I put on new clothes and rinsed my hair some, leaving the dirty clothes on the floor in the bathroom. Normally I wouldn't be such a slob, but I didn't want to turn the hamper into a fire hazard.

By the time I got back to the living room, Heather's mom was there in her bathrobe and tennis shoes. "It's out," she said to me. "Mr. Sanchez told me to tell you not to answer any questions till a fire marshal gets here."

"Where's Mr. TJ?" I demanded. "He needs to come here for the fire marshals, too."

"He's arguing with Mr. Sanchez, trying to get his briefcase out of the building."

"That's because his fire-setting stuff's in it," I said.

"Hush," said Mom, handing Ms. Sonntag a cup of coffee. "We can't talk about it yet."

"What else is there to talk about?" I asked.

"You could play race cars with me," suggested Sloop.

Not having anything better to do, I did. Mr. TJ came in after a bit, looking picked on. "I seem to be under constraint on my own property," he said. "May I borrow your phone to call my lawyer?"

"Sure," said Mom. "Your dad's on the way."

"You didn't drag him out of the office for this, did you?" said Mr. TJ, sounding appalled. "He's only been out of the hospital a little while. He doesn't need this excitement."

"His kid's been accused of arson," said Mom. "I know how that feels, as it happens. I wasn't going to hide it from him."

Mr. TJ looked sideways at me. "You know, Mrs. Wilson, there's no real harm done. The less fuss we make, the better for everyone, especially for Mary Jane. If you've already called the fire marshals, that can't be helped; but I'm sure we can keep things under control."

I looked up from pushing Sloop's Matchbox Corvette around the kitchen floor, and said, "You make me sick!"

"Me too!" said Sloop.

"Y'all," said Mom, in a warning voice.

"Well, he does," I said. "I thought you told the fire marshal you believe me."

"I did, and I do," said Mom, "but I don't know anything that justifies your being rude to anybody."

I guess grown-ups have to stick together on stuff like that.

I'm getting tired of writing about this. Most of the

126

story is already over, and the rest is just people talking. But I should tell you about Mr. Weller, and Mr. Sanchez, and what the other Burglars said when they got home, and then we'll be all done. My English teacher said she'd give me extra credit if I finish this by the end of the school year, so I guess I'll keep on. I usually get A's in English anyway, but I've never had an A plus, and that would be neat.

Mr. Weller and the fire marshals, Mr. Wyclaviak and Mr. Halliday, arrived about the same time. The right word for Mr. Weller is old. His face and his suits are all wrinkly (I think it's hard to keep a suit nice if you have to sit in a wheelchair, like he does), and he combs his hair over his bald spot. The first thing he did when he rolled in the door (which was hard; the doors are narrow and the wheelchair was wide) was look at Mr. TJ and say, "Is it true, boy?"

"I wish it weren't," said Mr. TJ, stretching his face in a sad look, "but I saw Mary Jane strike the match with my own eyes."

"You did not!" I protested. "Can't you even tell the truth to your own dad?"

"Now, now," said Mr. Wyclaviak, closing the apartment door behind Mr. Sanchez. Mr. Halliday was taking out a tape recorder. "We'll do this in an orderly fashion. You first, Sanchez."

I was getting tired of waiting around. "Why him first?" I asked. "I know a lot more about it."

"Hush," said Mom. "They know how they want to do it."

So Mr. Sanchez talked into the tape recorder, telling them all kinds of things they already knew, like his name and address and that he was a firefighter for such-and-such firehouse and this was his off time, or as he said his "downtime." This is a transcription of the interesting part of what he said:

At ten o'clock this morning, I received an anonymous phone call to the effect that the empty brick house near my apartment would be set fire to at some point today. I immediately went to consult with the apartment manager, Mrs. Wilson, and inspect the premises. I did not attempt to enter, since I had no warrant, and there were no signs of forced entry.

(On the tape you can hear me say, "Oh! So that's what you were doing!" and Mom hushing me and Sloop complaining he needs to go to the bathroom.)

Mrs. Wilson and I agreed that the call was probably a prank, but that it would be a good idea for both of us to keep an eye on the house.

Then he told how right after he ate his lunch he started to come out to check the Brick House again, and heard me yelling. We know all that. Then he talked about guarding the crime scene and finding the briefcase and the scorched apron.

Then it was Mr. TJ's turn. His lawyer had arrived, and whenever one of the marshals asked a question, he would look at the lawyer before answering. He also looked at his dad a lot. I got pretty antsy. Mr. TJ could fib like nobody's business, and I had to figure on Mr. Weller believing him. Since Mr. Weller is Mom's boss, that could be bad, even if the fire marshals believed me. And why should they? Mr. TJ was telling them, smoothly, without any hesitation or pauses, about finding the door unlocked ("My own carelessness," he admitted, as if he were embarrassed, but willing to take his little share of the blame) and seeing me light the match. Finally he finished, and Mr. Wyclaviak turned to me. "All right, Mary Jane, let's hear your version."

"May I go now?" asked Mr. TJ. "I'd like to take my father home."

"I'm fine," said Mr. Weller, looking first at him, then at me. He hadn't moved or spoken all this time, and hearing him sound so firm and stern made me even more nervous.

"There's business to attend to," said Mr. TJ.

"This is business," said Mr. Weller. "Sit down, boy."

Mr. TJ, who hadn't quite stood up, but had come to the edge of the couch, sat back.

And I started to talk.

CHAPTER SIXTEEN

End Pending

WELL, YOU KNOW WHAT ALL I TOLD THEM. WHEN I said what I'd done with the minutes book, Mr. Sanchez fetched it in, and the fire marshals looked it over. Mr. TJ changed color when they read out the last bit of it, that I wrote while waiting for him to show up; but then he shrugged and smiled. "She does have a vivid imagination," he said. "And you're good in English, aren't you, Mary Jane? It's natural to try to write stories about people you know, with yourself as the hero."

"Fortunately, everything in this book should be verifiable," said Mr. Wyclaviak. "We can question the other three girls, and the older children, independently."

"Oh, come now." Mr. TJ smiled. "It's plainly some elaborate game they were playing together. Of course they'll back Mary Jane, to keep her out of trouble."

"Marshall won't," Ms. Sonntag spoke up. "He's a terrible liar. It's too hard for him to remember what he's made up, so he always winds up with the truth."

Mr. Weller took the pipe he was chewing out of his mouth and looked at Mr. Sanchez. "The kittens," he said, "were they in the house?"

Mr. Sanchez nodded. "The mother cat had them all in the fireplace barricaded behind her body. The window seat was full of books and toys, too."

"Ah," said Mr. Weller, putting his pipe back into his mouth.

Mr. TJ opened his mouth, glanced at his lawyer, and said nothing.

All this talking went on forever. When it got to be time for Marshall to get home, Ms. Sonntag watched for him and brought him in to answer questions too. Then the other Burglars got home and ran in without knocking. "Well?" demanded Heather.

Before I could answer, Mr. Sanchez said, "What do you girls know about an anonymous phone call I got this morning?"

"Oh, that was us," said Heather. "Is it okay? Mary Jane's not in trouble, is she? If she is, I should be in trouble, too, because the Burglars were my fault."

"We should all be in trouble together," said Rainbow.

"But we shouldn't be in trouble at all, if Mary Jane was right," said Donnavita. "Was she right? Did you catch Mr. TJ?"

Mr. TJ changed color again. Mr. Weller looked at their faces, then at his son's face, then at his feet. Mr.

Halliday waved his hands. "Hush," he said. "You'll all have a chance to tell your stories."

"Why did you call Mr. Sanchez?" I asked. "I thought you didn't believe me."

"You never said enough for us to know whether we believed you or not," said Heather. "But we figured, you're such a wimp about being good all the time, you must have some great idea if you were willing to jump up and ditch school when we were all already grounded. So we thought we should give you some backup. If you'd waited another stop or two and explained, we might've come with you."

"Sorry," I said. I felt a lot less sick now.

About that time Mrs. Losoya came tearing down the sidewalk screaming in Spanish, and banged on our door. Mom had to let her in and calm her down, and the Wellers and the lawyer talked together under cover of all the noise. It turned out Mrs. Losoya'd just gotten a phone call telling her Jimmy had been arrested for selling drugs.

All this happened back in October. It's May now, almost time for school to let out, and a lot has happened.

First, the Brick House Burglars, even Rainbow, got grounded for a month. Even Domie said that breaking into the Brick House and not telling a grown-up about the danger of an arsonist was stupid and dangerous. I think Domie's feelings were kind of hurt that we'd never tried to tell her and Petal. It's not like they were

132

ordinary grown-ups and would have punished us, if we'd come straight to them. We just never thought of it.

Second, Jimmy Losoya and Los Red Dukes got arrested and charged with dope peddling. Some of them made bail and some of them didn't. Jimmy didn't, and he was so mad at the others for not chipping in and bailing him out that when he got out on probation, he cut up two or three of them with a switchblade, and got sent up again. He'd given all his money from the dope deals to his mom, and she'd spent it on rent and cheap wine. He's in juvenile hall now, and Mrs. Losoya skipped out without paying her last month's rent.

The funny thing is, between the time he got out on probation and the time he hurt his old friends, he came to see the Burglars. We came out of school one afternoon, and there he was, hanging out at the bus stop where we have to catch the bus. I guess we could've gone down a couple of blocks to the next one, but he could've followed us.

"He wants us to be scared," said Heather. "Act like you don't see him."

"What if he wants revenge for Roxanne helping turn him in?" I asked. "We'd better put Donnavita behind us."

So we did that, and walked up to the bus stop trying to be brave. I think Heather and Rainbow really were, but I would've run if I could've. Jimmy watched us coming, leaning against the pole that holds up the bus route sign.

"I heard y'all caught that snake Weller, trying to burn down his own house," he said, when we came up.

"Mary Jane did," said Rainbow.

"He tried to frame me, you know," said Jimmy.

"We know," said Rainbow. "He's trying to frame Mary Jane now."

Jimmy smiled. I'd never seen him do that before. He didn't look quite so scary when he smiled. "You kids are okay," he said. "You got guts. If you need me to testify anything against him, you just ask."

"What do you know about it?" asked Donnavita, surprised out of being scared.

Jimmy's smile changed, so that he looked scary again. "Nothing," he said, "but I'll say I know anything you want."

Heather turned red. "I don't think that'll be necessary," she said, primly.

"Whatever." He got on his motorbike and drove off, making too much noise, as usual. We all looked after him.

"You know, he could be good, if he wanted to," said Rainbow.

"Maybe he'll want to, now," I suggested.

But that same night he nearly killed three of Los Red Dukes, so I guess he doesn't.

The weirdest and most important thing that happened was that Mr. Weller came to tell us that he believed me, and not his son. He told Dad and Mom and me, sitting in the living room with Sloop pushing his dump truck around the floor. "I was in the hospital quite some time," he said, "and TJ had charge of the business. And he's made some bad choices. I've been going over the books. The insurance money from the Brick House and that adobe house that burned down would have about covered his losses. And the physical evidence backs Mary Jane, not him. The briefcase was empty except for some scraps of newspaper and a smell of turpentine. He didn't have anything he valued in that house, but Mary Jane had those things in the window seat and the kittens she wouldn't've wanted to burn. And that minutes book . . ." He shook his head. "I'm afraid it's pretty clear."

For some reason I felt worse than I had when we'd all thought he'd come to fire Mom. "But—he's your kid," I said.

"I know," said Mr. Weller. I don't know when I ever saw anyone look so unhappy. "I guess every bad apple in the world is somebody's kid. And maybe I'm not completely blameless myself." He shifted in his wheelchair. "Anyway, I'm retaining a lawyer for him, but I wanted y'all to know, I'm going to keep the pressure on for him to plead guilty and take his medicine. At least he didn't hire anybody else to do his dirty work for him—that's something. But trying to shove the blame onto a child . . ." He shook his head again.

"He took care not to hurt anyone, anyhow," said Dad. "He could have set that fire a lot more safely and surely at night, when we were all asleep and less likely either to notice him, or to get out before it spread to the apartments."

"That's so," said Mr. Weller. "I guess I could have more to be ashamed of." But he didn't sound any happier. "I've got to pay for the lawyer—y'all can see that. But I want to make up to you for all the trouble you've had. So I've come to tell you, I'm going to go ahead and renovate the Brick House."

I clapped my hands. Mom and Dad smiled. Sloop drove his dump truck into the back of Mr. Weller's wheelchair, and I had to drag him off to his room. When I got back, Mr. Weller was saying, "Of course, I never have allowed pets in this building, but there's that mama cat and all those kittens. The kids are still feeding them, as far as I know. If that's not pets, I don't know what you'd call it."

"Of course we're still feeding them," I said. "Don't make us chase them out! It's almost winter, and they'll get cold and starve and—"

Dad motioned me to hush. "That's not what he's talking about."

Suddenly I felt hopeful. "What are you talking about then?"

"I don't think much of anybody who'd have a dog in a place like this," Mr. Weller said, "but cats, guinea pigs, like that, what're they going to do but rip up the carpet? And the carpet gets spoiled if you let kids in, anyhow. So why shouldn't we let in pets, starting with Isis and family?"

So that's why we all have cats now. Bib for me, Boots for Heather, Sunshine for Donnavita, Nyota for Rainbow, and Isis for Marshall. Having a cat in your own house is about a million times better than having one in a separate building. There won't be any more kittens, though, because Mr. Weller talked to us very seriously about the cat overpopulation problem, and we took them in to be fixed.

Men're working on the Brick House right now. There's going to be video games, and Ping-Pong, and a room for parties, and Petal will quit her job, which was lousy anyway, and run a day-care center for apartment children. Mr. Weller says if Marshall wants to be janitor he can. It's the sort of job he can do, if he doesn't have to fix the furnace or anything like that.

Roxanne isn't sweet on Mr. Sanchez anymore. She found out he and Mr. Anstruther are sort of married to each other. Roxanne is mad about it and doesn't like him anymore, but the rest of us do. He had T-shirts made for us that say "The Brick House Burglars" on the front, and our names on the backs. They're way cool, just like football shirts.

I can't really end the story, because we haven't had Mr. TJ's trial yet. He refuses to plead guilty and acts real hurt that his dad won't believe him and fired him from the business. Mr. Wyclaviak says trials take a long time, so I might could be almost grown-up before I get to testify in court, telling the truth the whole truth so help me God and all that. I didn't want to forget any of it, so I've written it all out with help from the others and a photocopy of the minutes book that the fire marshals let me have—the real minutes book is evidence. I can't end the story, but I think everything'll be all right, and I pretty much have to stop here.

I hope it's enough to get me an A plus in English.